HACKED FOR LOVE

A BILLIONAIRE ROMANCE

MICHELLE LOVE

CONTENTS

1. Chapter 1		1
2. Chapter 2		9
3. Chapter 3		15
4. Chapter 4		22
5. Chapter 5		30
6. Chapter 6		37
7. Chapter 7		44
8. Chapter 8		56
9. Chapter 9		63
10. Chapter 10		72
11. Chapter 11		78
12. Chapter 12		87

Made in "The United States" by:

Michelle Love

© Copyright 2020 – Michelle Love

ISBN: 978-1-64808-210-8

ALL RIGHTS RESERVED. No part of this publication may be reproduced or transmitted in any form whatsoever, electronic, or mechanical, including photocopying, recording, or by any informational storage or retrieval system without express written, dated and signed permission from the author

❦ Created with Vellum

Brilliant, reclusive young hacker Robin Locke just pulled off the score of the century. She has successfully hacked the Bitcoin wallets of multiple billionaires and left electronic "breadcrumbs" for each of the three men to find, implicating each other's IT departments for the theft. Armed with almost a billion dollars in stolen funds, she's poised to change the lives of fifty thousand desperate Americans through anonymous donations.

Unfortunately for Robin, one of the three billionaires—and the only one not connected to a crime family—has seen *A Fistful of Dollars* and knows this gambit when he sees it. Drake Steele, Bitcoin billionaire turned successful industrialist, is determined to find the hacker who stole from him, and not only get back his money, but get a very angry mafioso off his back. But when he finally tracks her down, he ends up with an unexpected dilemma.

CHAPTER 1

Robin

I can't sleep again. There's too much crying outside. And it's kids this time, which makes it that much worse.

I glance up from my wall-length computer desk over to the window where the noise is trickling through. The drama across the alley started two hours ago and just keeps going. I'm not mad at the miserable family making the racket; they can't help it.

I'm mad at the one who made them miserable.

This bastard Tom Link is just like my uncle. Those poor tenants.

After learning about all the slumlords in this neighborhood, I decided to do something about it. I've started buying up the buildings around here, fixing them up and making sure the rent's fair, the hot water runs, and the lights don't flicker every time someone runs a space heater. I hire a long-term tenant to be the building manager, and over time a shitty place becomes a decent one.

But I haven't gotten to that one next door yet. The owner wants too much for the building; I have to find a way to make him desperate enough to knock the price down. I do not want him walking away with a small fortune when he should be dragged off in chains.

It won't be tough—like most guys with pockets as deep as his, Thomas Link must have skeletons in his closet. And I know I can yank the door wide open. All I need is something juicy enough—outstanding warrants, tax evasion.

MY FINGERS START DANCING over the keyboard again as I glower at my screen. Around me, my dim apartment is warm and snug; double windows, extra insulation, and a hydronic heating system were just a few of the improvements I made to this building.

I still remember how it feels to sleep in a cardboard box. Now when I crank up the temperature to seventy-five degrees, I feel like I'm overindulging.

But this is what everyone deserves. And I've been trying to make sure that everyone has it—on the dime of those who are so ridiculously rich that they'll never miss it. Every year, I get a little further along in making this dark, crumbling corner of South Park, Seattle a better place to live.

I'll find something to break Link, and then go in and fix that building, too.

If Tom Link's public face is this nasty, chances are he is five times worse in private. *Get the right information to the right people, and he'll be begging for ready cash to defend himself in court.* I smile frostily at my screen as I type.

Link refuses to spend a cent to upgrade the building infrastructure, even when ordered to by the city. Right now, their "free heat," an ancient set of radiators that I can usually hear banging away from my bedroom, isn't working.

Which means a whole building full of tenants are now huddled around space heaters, wrapped up in blankets, trying to tough out this epic cold snap. And some of them are going hungry, too. *That prick. He must know—he just doesn't care.*

I WILL NEVER in my life understand people who just don't care.

And that's why I'm going to punish him—and steal some of his resources to start fixing this problem. *Book them all into hotels? Buy them all down comforters and low-wattage heaters?* I'll come up with something; I always do.

When I was a little girl and Mom and Dad were still alive, they would have the driver take us through the worst neighborhoods back in D.C. and Baltimore. They did this to show me the struggles of poor people and to show me how to reach out a hand to help. It taught me gratitude for what I had and sympathy for those with nothing.

And then I had nothing, not even my parents, and I started sympathizing with poorer people even more. More than that—thanks to what my remaining "family" did, I started hating wealthy predators and the damage they do to the world.

A family out there is going without dinner. The father is angry and apologetic. The mother weeps in shame.

I'll send them something. But how do I figure out which apartment they're in?

It's January now—deep winter. After the holidays, the food banks around here run dry for a while, and everyone's already behind on their bills. So, little kids all over town end up going hungry, and their parents are blamed for not being richer.

To hell with it. Everyone around here could use some help.

I order pizza, wings, juice, and hot coffee for the whole building on the landlord's account. Then I make myself tea and sit down to brainstorm about what else I can do for them before I manage to buy the place.

Compassion is a heavy burden—but I would rather bear it than be a complete piece of shit like Link.

Half an hour after I put in the huge order, I go to the window to wait and listen. Eventually, I hear surprised exclamations, and the crying dries up. Meanwhile, every light in the building is now on. A peek down the alley shows at least two delivery cars parked at its mouth.

The misery is gone, replaced by a contented silence as little tummies are filled. For a while after that, even in the middle of this bleak-ass winter, I actually feel all right.

It's one of the rules I live by. If you want the world to be a better place, go out and do something about it. If the law won't let you, figure out a way. Break the law—rob from the rich, save a life. Save fifty.

Whenever I help someone using money some rich guy won't miss, I know I'm on the right track, because afterward, I can sleep. In the morning, the world seems less crappy for a while, and I can live with myself better, too.

Money alone could never do that for me. My parents understood that, and so do I.

The loneliness? Well, that's another thing. I've spent a lot of time in isolation, even after I was off the streets. There's something about being a street kid that makes it hard to connect with people again when the opportunity comes back.

That's me, now. I watch over people. I don't make friends with them.

I hear talking and laughter over across the alley now. Someone's faintly playing classic rock. A kid giggles.

I let out a soft sigh of relief and sit back in my desk chair, which creaks a little stiffly. I still don't feel the least bit sleepy, and I find my eyes drifting over to a folder at the top of my computer desktop.

I've still got that cold feeling in the pit of my stomach that tells me I'm still a little upset, and that even if I could sleep, I won't rest. I'll spend the rest of the night reliving the winter I spent on the streets of Baltimore with the organ music from my parents' double funeral still echoing in my head.

The folder is labeled "A Fistful of Bitcoin," referencing one of my favorite movies, and the currency involved in the heist. The plan within will be the biggest, most daring, and most life-saving operation that I have ever come up with…if I actually go through with it.

I have a database of twenty thousand people in the greater Seattle area whose lives could be completely turned around with a windfall of just fifty thousand dollars. Medical bills, college debt, back mortgages, credit cards, fines, homelessness—each one of them is struggling with something. I can help them all—as long as I'm willing to risk making some truly dangerous enemies.

If I go through with it, it will all start with a massive Bitcoin heist against three very deserving targets. Bitcoin. I chose this because it's the currency I've started doing all my transactions with, so I know the ins and outs of the system—and because most of my targets do not even know if they own a lot of it.

As for the one target who does know…his security is good, but it's not as good as he thinks it is.

There are eight "traditional" billionaires in the greater Seattle area: famous, well-known captains of industry. There are three Bitcoin billionaires who made their fortunes recently by investing in Bitcoin cryptocurrency right before its enormous rise in value. Two of these men could probably buy up most of the rest, but only because they each run a piece of the local underworld.

Every last one of them—like my uncle, like Link, like so many others—is an unethical, lying, cash-grubbing piece of work. Between them, they have bought their way out of so many criminal charges and massive fines that I hate thinking about it. Even Drake Steele, one of the Bitcoin billionaires, and a guy heavily into funding local small businesses, has a history of doing large scale money laundering for a certain *someone* starting a decade back.

Drake is the second target I picked for my heist. He is one of three men presumed to be criminal, each likely to have a territorial beef with the others, and each likely to be led to suspect one another for the cryptocurrency theft I'm making off with. While they're bickering, I can make sure their money gets quietly sent where it will do the most good. The whole plan relies on them blaming each other for the theft.

Each one has decent security on their Bitcoin wallets and other online repositories. Steele's security has given me some problems, but I've dipped into them for unnoticeable amounts multiple times. This is just a bigger bite—and just like the Man with No Name, I'll leave the bad guys blaming each other for the trouble I cause. Maybe they'll even kill each other off.

Cyber hacks like this are my specialty: the slow, subtle drain of resources; the big, showy hit to the wallet that someone else gets blamed for. I could be a billionaire myself by now, if I was selfish enough to keep that money.

BUT THAT'S NOT ME. My wealth redistribution is a straight up public service—and often in amounts that billionaires would still consider negligible.

They're not my only targets, either. Plenty of embezzlers have found their stolen funds vanishing out from under them, while a local grandma gets a new roof.

I sigh through my nose and open the dossier on Steele. Drake Steele, youngest of the three by decades, has a mysterious background and no known relatives. He prefers to fund incubators instead of pay taxes—which is a lot better than not paying at all.

Also, hot. Disgustingly, distractingly hot.

I switch to his photo folder and drink in his images *again*. This is the man I'm contemplating relieving of fifty thousand Bitcoin—which translates to hundreds of millions of dollars.

I don't know anything about intimacy with men, but I know to be wary of ones that I can't look away from. I could stare at Drake Steele for minutes at a stretch as I wonder what he looks like under that nice suit—just from a picture. That kind of magnetism alarms me.

I have to make sure that we never actually meet.

Still, looking at a man like that makes me want to dream a little. Tall and muscular, with the sharp, noble features of a Roman statue, pale skin, wavy mahogany-colored hair that reaches his jawline, and ice-gray eyes. *What a waste.*

I catch myself yawning, and I sigh in relief, getting up from my desk and stretching. Maybe I'm relaxed enough now from the night's successes to get an actual nap in.

I prefer to sleep through sunrise. There's something uniquely depressing about facing the dawn alone, even if I have done it since I was ten.

I'm still pulling together the last details on this project. I have time to decide whether to actually go through with it. A slow and steady draining of their wallets would be safer, but I'm torn.

There are so many people in this town who need help, and they need it soon.

I'll sleep on it, I think as I strip off my sweater and wander to bed in my yoga pants and a black tank top. I pull my hair off my shoulders and tie it up with a plain elastic band before clambering into bed.

Strangely, the last thing in my head before I doze off is Steele's beautiful face and cold eyes. I want to ask him when he stopped caring about people, but as I drop off, I remind myself again of the rules I've set.

We must never meet.

2
CHAPTER 2

Drake

I should know by now never to go through the news feeds during breakfast. It always shows the most depressing shit. And this morning, as I sit in my breakfast nook in one corner of my penthouse, is no exception.

My bagel with lox, cream cheese, and purple tomatoes sits there untouched as I stare gloomily at the touchscreen in front of me. It rests in a plain black stand partway across the table. Wary of getting crumbs on it, I use an extra-long stylus to flick through article after article describes disasters, crime, government corruption, and people near and far being fucked over.

I stop at one in particular and let out a heavy sigh before forcing myself to choke down some orange juice as I skim over the article. *Every time I read about this goddamn fire in South Park the situation gets more screwed up.*

The tragedy hit the news on an icy night three days ago.

There's a whole little list of headlines, which outline the story pretty well by themselves:

Electrical Fire in South Park Leaves Three Dead, Scores Homeless

South Park Fire Casualties Now at Five

Electrical System Overloaded After Tenants Forced to Use Space Heaters

Landlord Questioned Over Unheated Building

Fire Marshall Discovers Disconnected Sprinkler System, Fire Hoses

Self-Described "Frugal" South Park Slumlord Hit with Multiple Violations

South Park Slumlord May Face Wrongful Death Lawsuits, Lawyers Up

The list isn't even done yet, and I already have a headache. I turn the screen away from me to concentrate on my breakfast, cutting my eyes toward the view outside as I scoop up my loaded bagel and bite into it like a burger. The burst of flavor on my tongue wakes me a little from my doldrums, and I grunt in satisfaction, giving a little nod.

The world's misery can wait until I have a full stomach and a focused mind.

The view outside reminds me of the Northeast or maybe even back home: white rooftops, evergreens crowned with snow dotting bleak hills full of bare broadleafs, plows beeping as they push the mess down on the street into piles at the side of the road. Now and again, I hear the screech-honk-crunch of a fender bender as wheels slide out of control on patches of ice.

This winter has been brutal. After two strangely mild early Februaries in a row, we're now breaking records in the other direction.

Which is why everyone had their electric heaters blasting in that apartment building. No radiators. Just trying to stay warm in some antiquated shit-heap with an electrical system that probably hasn't been upgraded since the fifties.

I wince and force myself to bite down on my bagel again, chewing angrily. I can't afford to get this caught up in other people's problems. My family used to mock me for being too soft-hearted.

And they had a point—unplanned, emotional decisions cause nothing but trouble. I have my own ways of working for the greater good, and they don't involve swooping in to rescue every desperate person I run across. If they have a plan for pulling themselves out of poverty, then I'll help them in a second, but I'm no hero.

I finish my bagel, my collagen drink, and half my orange juice before I let myself look back at my flat screen. The latest additions to the stories make me lift an eyebrow; the newest posting is barely an hour old.

Donation Site for South Park Fire Victims Receives $25k In Three Days

South Park Slumlord Facing Wrongful Death Lawsuits from Victims' Families

South Park Slumlord Attacks Fire Marshall During Questioning, Jailed

I sit back, a faint smile of relief on my face. *Good. A bit of a happy ending. These people don't need my help now—someone else took care of it.*

My phone rings suddenly as I'm downing the last of my orange juice. I tense slightly, realizing it's the front desk. I'm not expecting any visitors for hours.

I scoop it up and connect the call. "This had better be good, Grayson," I grumble at the building's security supervisor.

"I'm sorry, sir," he replies in a slightly strained voice. "But Ms. Siddiq and Mr. Castleton are here together to see you. They say it's urgent."

My eyebrows climb. My head of IT *and* head of security showing up for an emergency face-to-face? *That is a really bad sign.* "Let them up at once."

I'm still in my shirtsleeves as I leave the breakfast area, cuffs rolled to my elbows, brushing a few crumbs off my vest. Whatever is going on, I'll handle it. I've never faced a challenge I couldn't meet.

Twenty minutes later, though, I'm dealing with something that hits me a lot closer to home than an apartment fire in the bad part of town. "How much did they take?"

Laura Siddiq, a tiny woman whose round face, large brown eyes, and nervous movements remind me of a chipmunk, has handled my IT since I first made my fortune five years ago. She also handles security and upkeep for my Bitcoin wallets, miners, and accounts, which is why she has a look of horror on her face right now.

John Castleton, meanwhile, looks a little frustrated, and I can't blame him. He handles the physical security of my home, businesses, and fortune, which doesn't allow him to help much in a situation like this. He's a dapper mountain of a man with a shaved head that gleams like ebony and a coiled-spring look to him, like a tense panther.

"Twenty-five hundred Bitcoin in total," Laura sighs out nervously, her fingers knotting together in her lap.

That is a third of a billion fucking dollars. The cold fact of the robbery sinks in like a stone in my gut—and when it hits the bottom, anger blooms.

It's not even a tenth of my *liquid* assets. Barely a bite. But it's the first time that someone has dared to steal from me, and I'm suddenly ready to kick some ass.

"Any leads?" I continue in a stony voice, and Laura flinches slightly...then blinks and relaxes slightly, as if she'd been expecting me to fire her right off.

"Well, whoever it was is brilliant. You know how good our cybersecurity is—we worked together to create it. But this person slipped in like a ghost through a wall. There aren't even traces of their entry into the system." She relaxes slightly as she sees me calm a little.

"How the hell did someone blow past all our hard work like it was nothing?" It hurts my pride to think that there's someone out there better at hacking than I am. But then again, I haven't been in the game for years, except to protect my own systems with Laura's help.

"I have no idea. I have half our team trying to find the security breach while the rest tries to find and track any transaction confirmations for those particular Bitcoins in the blockchain. Finding out where the money went and tracking it through the block records will help us figure out who took it."

"Uh," John sits forward. "Sorry for being out of my depth, but could someone translate that for me?"

I nod curtly. "Bitcoin have a decentralized database called the blockchain, which records every transaction that a specific Bitcoin goes through. It makes it easier to trace them and harder to duplicate them."

That catches his interest. "So, all we have to do is trace who uses them next?"

"Theoretically," Laura says honestly enough. "There are ways around the blockchain, and Bitcoin can be converted into other currency. Once that happens, tracking it becomes problematic."

"But not impossible," John replies.

"No," I reply in that same firm tone. "Absolutely not impossible—not for us."

I LOOK between the two of them. "Here's the deal. I want to know where my money went and who had their hands on it. John, once we find out who is behind this, I trust you to retrieve this person so that he and I can have a little chat."

They both nod, and I stand to see them out. "Let's get it done."

Someone is going to pay for this.

CHAPTER 3

Robin

It's been three days since I've slept. Three days since screams woke me and I came out to see the neighboring building on fire. It was worse than I thought—no sprinkler system and walls full of dry rot. The place went up like a torch.

So now there's no building to buy.

My tenants and I were pulling people out of that smoky mess well before the fire department rolled up. I opened up my lobby to give everyone a warm place to gather and wait for ambulances. I put the people with no place to go up in hotels, paying for it with stolen funds from Link's accounts again.

Because fuck him—all of this is his fault. Except...except for the part where I could have just given him what he wanted. That choice I made—to make sure he wouldn't benefit too much from the sale of the building, instead of prioritizing the safety of his tenants—will haunt me for the rest of my life.

I spent the first day shuffling whoever I could from the burned building into vacancies in my buildings, getting victim assistance and insurance for everyone I could, trying to keep the guilt and horror at bay with action. These people needed help, and I was going to be there for them.

Then I found out about the deaths.

I should have just given that fucker what he was asking and taken over sooner.

I've been a wreck since then. I've been working myself to the bone—too much work, too little rest, food, or time away from the keyboard. I know I've gotten obsessive and that I'm hurting myself. But I can't stop.

That was the state I was in when I finally set the Fistful of Bitcoins heist in motion before dawn today. Choosing to do it at that moment probably wasn't my best decision either. I was way too unfocused and emotional.

I still feel that way now, even after running errands for this mission all day. But when I started, I was downright distraught.

I definitely wasn't thinking of the danger to me. I'm still not. But as I doze off in my chair in front of my main computer screen, I can't shake a nagging worry that I might have created more problems than solutions with my heist.

It's crazy. I've spent weeks covering every angle on this plan, thinking through every weakness—but my gut doesn't know that. My instincts are used to a world where unfair horror, tragedy, and betrayal can drop on your head at any moment. I don't trust this success.

I've already started buying some necessities for a few of the people on my list. Time to start getting people their money and killing their debts now—before the hunt for me can even begin. I'm still hoping that any potential search for me will be futile and will lead all three men to the wrong conclusions—and to each other—instead.

If they find me, it won't be until it's too late. They are going to help these innocent people survive whether they want to or not. And then if I die, I die.

First though, I need to check on how well the fund for my neighbors is doing. I log onto the donation site I set up and check—and lean back suddenly, my eyes going wide.

What the hell?

There's a quarter of a million dollars just chilling in the account. It was thirty thousand earlier today—impressive enough, but this is amazing. I quickly check the donor list—and end up even more shocked and confused.

Drake Steele, $200,000, donated an hour ago.

No. Fucking. Way.

A man like him can afford to drop two hundred thousand dollars on pretty much anything, just for fun. I know that both the fire and all the scandals I have unleashed on Link as punishment have been all over the news. *Did it actually make Steele feel bad?*

Even if it's just a coincidence that he chose to donate to the one fund that I set up...Steele supports businesses, not people. He's got no public record of being charitable outside of his incubators, and though those are helpful, they are largely a tax dodge.

Unless, of course, my research on him is incomplete. Flawed. *Have I missed something?*

Did he find me out that fast, and is this his way of telling me? Or does this guy have a secret life, doing the kinds of things my parents used to do?

I suddenly feel sick. Drake Steele got his start as a money launderer for "unknown interests." He was a scumbag with all sorts of whispers about his past.

But is he a scumbag *now*? Maybe he didn't just get better at covering his tracks, as I had assumed, but actually *changed*. If that's true, then he's the only billionaire I have ever seen who has managed to reform himself instead of getting more corrupt over time.

And if that's the case, then I may have just made him some deadly enemies that he doesn't deserve!

I sit back in my chair, huffing softly, my blood gone cold. *Should I send him a warning?*

It means giving away the scheme to one of my targets. It may even mean ruining my whole plan if he comes after me hard enough. But if he's not the man I thought he was, then I'll have his death on my conscience.

I have enough deaths on my conscience already.

I set up a crawler program to quietly gather data from donation sites about Steele's activities. If he is making a lot of donations like this, even if he's doing it under variants of his name or one of the pseudonyms I already found, the crawler will dig them up.

Meanwhile, I can start doing my real work, praying that I can settle my mind a little with some more altruistic therapy.

I have randomized my list of needy people. I know it's going to take me a hell of a lot of time to get everything handled, but I have a lot of money to parcel out and I need it to happen fast. I wish I had some help at this, but as with everything else, I'm working alone.

The first name is Lois Pinoy. She's a hospital nurse who has ended up on disability leave because of tendon issues in her arm caused by turning patients twice her size for years. Widowed mom of three. I bring up her photograph and look into the face of a petite woman in pink scrubs, smiling tiredly while standing behind her small, grinning son's wheelchair.

Her eyes are very gentle.

"Hi there, Lois." I smile at the screen, feeling a little sense of connection that eases a deep hollowness inside me. "This is the wealth-redistribution fairy coming at you with a big dose of hope and help."

She uses the same password for everything. That makes it easy for me to get into places that a black-hat hacker would maliciously take advantage of. Bank accounts, mortgage account, medical accounts. I wish I could drop her a note somewhere telling her not to do that, but I have to move as invisibly as possible.

She owes the bank for her little, ramshackle house, which is also in need of repairs. She's deep in the red on credit cards, and by the looks of her purchases, she's just trying to get by while she can't work. Her son's medical debt doesn't help; he needs physical therapy and prosthetic lower legs that she can't pay for.

Total need: $128,000.

Paying off those debt records and arranging for the prosthetics, fittings, and physical therapy all do my heart good. I even manage to get my mind off of Steele for a while.

In the past I've tried just going into the hospital and bank systems of people in trouble and changing the numbers, but the discrepancy is always caught and corrected. Now, though, someone is actually paying off those bills with real money. It's just not a someone anyone would expect.

Fifteen minutes from when I first entered her accounts, I print out one double-sided page on Lois and what was done for her and her family before purging her information from my system. Then I move onto the next random person.

Michael LaFloret, a medical cannabis user picked up just over state lines with a legally bought ounce. Released upon full legalization, but his record stands. Can't get a job now that he's free.

Michael wants to start his own business, but first he has to get out of the red with his landlord who is about to throw him into the streets in the middle of winter. I pay off his debts and pad his account by $10k, which is the maximum gift amount he can get in a year without being taxed on it.

Total need: $14,000.

Godspeed, Michael, and I hope you get your bike shop up and running.

It goes on like that. It doesn't take me long to fix someone's financial problems, print their file, clear them from my system and move on—as long as I keep focused. Fortunately, that's not difficult; if anything, I'm *too* focused.

Some take under five minutes. Others: half an hour. Many of the individuals on the list are parts of a larger family, which means I can clear up to ten at one go. Others are alone, which is the source of some of their problems.

I can sympathize.

It's going to take months to go through all this even if I devote twelve to fifteen hours a day to it. I may get caught before it's done or even killed. But I won't give up until I'm done—they'll have to drag me away from my list and what I'm trying to do.

This is giving me life even as it gives them life. For once, I matter. I'm not just my uncle's throwaway girl. I'm important to these people, and what I do matters—even if nobody ever knows my name.

I save a hundred people in a few hours, and then I start sending out e-mails about the fire fund's success to my former neighbors. They need to start getting their money and supplies, too.

It's getting light outside, and my head is throbbing before I finally sit back and stretch, yawning hard. I think I might actually be able to get some sleep now. But as I look up at the folder in the corner of my screen, I know I have something to check on first.

When I do, I swear under my breath.

The crawler search on Drake Steele has dug up scores of

entries. He's been making private donations to people—well away from venture support—to the tune of millions per fiscal quarter for at least half a decade.

Guilt money? It doesn't matter. What matters is that he's already doing the right thing, at least more than I've ever seen his kind do, and I just punished him anyway. And now, he could die.

I let out a little sob of dismay, covering my mouth with my hand as the screen blurs in front of me. *Oh god, I fucked up.*

How did this happen? I was so careful. Was I biased in choosing him because of his past? Or is it because he's just so annoyingly...perfect, as well as being rich?

I squeeze my eyes shut, horrified with myself but determined to fix this. *Focus.*

One last thing to do before my exhausted body forces me to bed, so I can rest without nightmares. I create an untraceable e-mail account; I put Drake Steele's private e-mail address in the recipient field; and I send him the damn warning.

I'd rather die myself than risk getting a decent man killed.

4

CHAPTER 4

Drake

The exercise yard is a blank gray box without a roof. We can just barely see the tops of the tallest Siberian pines on the outside if we look, but no one ever does. We're too busy watching each other.

If you put too many of even the gentlest animals together in too small of a cage, they will start fighting. Convicts are not gentle animals. And there are a hundred men stuffed into this yard, which was built for about fifty.

I'm the youngest man in there—still a boy, really—not that anyone cares. My skin is a blank slate—no needle has touched it yet and no knife. That's about to change, but not because I invited it.

My cousin had told me to ride my bike around the neighborhood and keep watch while he sold something I never saw. When the police roared up, I thought they were there for something else—until they shot at him. Now he is dead, and though I never knew why I was watching things for Leonid, they tried me as an adult.

Now I am here alone in this prison for killers.

Don't you dare look scared, *I remind myself. I walk quietly around the edge of the yard, not getting too near anyone, just trying to stretch my legs while my breath steams around me and occasional snowflakes drift past my face. I can feel dozens of icy stares on my back.*

Heavy bootsteps trail behind me. I tense and stop, squashing myself against the fence, praying that the owner of the boots will pass and go his own way—away from me.

"Hey. Kid."

Sick with terror, I turn around, trying to remind myself: I have done nothing. I have offended no one. *"Yes, sir?"*

I look up into a scarred, grinning face with an uneven beard and then feel a hard blow to my gut. I stare up at him in shock as I double over, completely confused. He's laughing and so are his friends.

The bruising feeling spreads, accompanied by cold nausea. My hands are getting wet where I hold myself. I watch him walk back to his friends, still wondering why he's done this, and I see him toss the bloody shiv over the fence and wipe off his hand...

I wake up holding my scar, letting out a little shout as I sit up. I orient myself almost instantly, but my heart keeps pounding. "Unh...shit," I mutter, waiting for my breath to even out before reaching for my water glass.

I guess I shouldn't be surprised, I think as I swallow the water down without tasting it. It puts a small dent in my headache, but I know it will take a while for the throbbing in my temples to clear. If I get stressed enough, the nightmares come back, and all my skill with lucid dreaming won't let me grab control of them.

Right now, I'm pretty damned stressed. I'm pissed off, but I don't have a face to punch yet. Nothing that has been uncovered about the Bitcoin theft makes any sense at all, and after a whole day of searching, we're no closer to finding out who is behind it.

My staff is focusing on two transactions. Temporarily,

someone actually swelled my accounts by almost eighty thousand Bitcoin, before sending that—plus twenty-five thousand of my own Bitcoin—on to someone else. The troubling parts are the names—of my unexpected donor and of the person who apparently stole from me on that same night.

Don Rocco Marcone, a violent bastard with a brain like a brick, is the supposed donor. And Dr. Taki Yoshida, the quietly effective local oyabun, is the supposed thief—which makes no goddamned sense at all.

Yoshida is not a thief. And Marcone would never send me money, so he'll likely end up thinking that I stole from him. Also, twenty-five thousand of the Bitcoin dumped into my account from Marcone belonged to Yoshida before that. *Round and round it goes...and I'll bet after the stop in Yoshida's accounts, it gets withdrawn and vanishes.*

I look at the open notebook beside me, which has a triangle with arrows drawn in it. The money moves from account to account and snowballs as it goes, then zaps off in an arrow without a label on it yet. I blame Yoshida; Yoshida blames Marcone; and Marcone blames me. We fight...while someone else makes off with our money.

Where have I seen this plot before? It seems awfully familiar.

Get people to fight each other while you make off with their money. The name of the movie's on the tip of my tongue. The circumstances are a lot different, but the principle's the same.

I take a deep breath and get up to put on my track pants. I used to like just cranking up the heat and exercising nude, or nearly. But after being the cause of an almost fatal distraction for a female window-washer, I now at least wear something over my bottom half.

Though for all I know, she might have just wanted to count all the marks on my skin.

To gain the favor of a *bratva* you must do many things. The brotherhood of thieves has no tolerance for cowards, for betrayers, for those who take from them and give back nothing. I was sixteen when I got my first tattoo, even before the stitches in my belly were taken out.

I look down at the formerly black and white design wrapped over my bicep: a rose coiled around a dagger. Its original outline had been gouged into my skin with home-mixed ink on the tip of a needle that had been fastened to an electric shaver. It had taken twenty hours in two long, painful sessions. I was told that if I cried, they would kill me instead of taking me underwing.

My eyes stayed bone-dry, though I almost bit through my lip. They were impressed. Then they found out that I have a natural talent for math, computers, and money, and they were even more impressed.

They put me to work as soon as I was processed out—which took four years, even though my conviction was eventually thrown out. I never went back to prison after that; my new family instead sent me away from Russia and to the States to handle a local *bratva* leader's money. I trained my mind as brutally as I had my body, getting rid of my Muscovite accent and learning everything I could about computers and finance.

The whole time, I put aside what they paid me as often as I could, looking for something to invest in that would free me from them. That's where my seed money came from. I'm not proud of it, but a man has to survive, and I had no control over my fate until I repaid my debt to them.

I warm up with some yoga in my home gym, which takes up a quarter of my penthouse's lower floor, and then hop on the elliptical for some cardio. The walls of the gym are mirrored so I can check my form; sometimes, the tall, tattooed brute in the mirror startles me a little.

He doesn't seem like me. He's not the man my employees

know—but then again, none of them have seen me under my suit.

I remember defending my brothers with a shiv in the prison yard, and I remember paying for my freedom by laundering massive amounts of cash for the *bratva*. But just like everything else that happened to me, from the day the Moscow police picked me up, until I started my new life half a decade ago, none of it seems like my life. It was more like an act I had to carry on at until I had earned my way out and I could live again.

So, half the time when I look in those mirrors, I expect to see that skinny, hungry, oblivious kid who didn't even have the sense to ride away when the police pulled into his neighborhood.

I'm burning up the miles on my elliptical, arms and legs pumping, a sheen of sweat rising on my skin. I have more scars now than tattoos, the stiff, leathery patches of skin growing thinner and smoother after years of treatment, but still pulling in spots as my muscles strain.

The belly wound. Defensive scars on the outsides of my arms. A slash across my back. And the patches where, by request, I removed some of the tattoos that signified my membership and rank in the *bratva*.

You don't just get to buy your way out, even though I handed over to them the first billion that I ever made.

The cross on my chest they'd wanted taken off the old-fashioned way: with the rough side of a brick. I stood there and scraped it off myself as they held a funeral for me, knowing that if I failed to sever ties correctly then I would fill the coffin they had brought. The bow tie with the dollar sign across my collarbones is gone now, too; the flesh is still a little raw. That one, like the stars on my shoulders, they let me remove normally.

The rose and knife, the dove with the olive branch over my heart, and the snarling skull on my shoulder I'd had colored by a professional once the others were all gone. Now they remind me of my past, without looking too much like prison tattoos. As unreal as that time feels, I must never forget it.

I've changed my life—hell, I've even changed my name—but I will never allow myself to forget how I got to where I am.

My cellphone chirps at me: Laura. I connect the video call before going back to puffing away. "Good morning! What have you got for me?"

"Our thief is spending and trading at least some of the stolen Bitcoin off the blockchain." Her announcement is an exasperated sigh, sounding just a touch tinny because she's put me on speakerphone.

"In English!" John grumbles in the background, and I snort.

"You can take Bitcoin and load them onto a hard drive, a thumb drive, or other device, and trade or spend them offline at a lot of brick and mortar stores these days especially in major urban centers. If you do that, those Bitcoin stay out of the system until the store spends them again, at which point they re-enter the blockchain and their movements start being recorded again. It's called a cold-wallet purchase."

"So, it's like walking around with cash. Until that money gets put back into someone else's account the banking system doesn't recognize it." John nods slowly, brows drawn together.

I hear Laura sipping tea. "Mmhmm! That is what I have been monitoring for—the moment any of our missing Bitcoin pop up again."

This is starting to sound hopeful. "And some of them have?" I ask in a controlled tone.

Laura sounds excited despite her obvious exhaustion. "Yes, as of fifteen minutes ago. And right here in Seattle, too."

"Who would do this?" I mutter. I didn't leave behind enemies in the *bratva,* or much of anywhere as far as I know. So why is this happening?

"I've been going through a list of potential suspects with

John over breakfast," Laura says a little distractedly as she types. "None of them have enough interest in technology to pull this off or would even know who to hire to pull this off."

They're having breakfast together? I dismiss the thought with a little shake of my head. "Forget that. Maybe we should stop focusing on who I might have pissed off and look instead at how the money is being used."

"You think that maybe the thief's got a cause in mind?" John muses.

"If whoever is behind this is taking this big a risk by spending any of the money this soon, there has to be some urgency behind it."

More typing, and then Laura gasps slightly as I keep marching away on my elliptical.

"What is it?" I puff, muscles straining. The stripe of scar tissue across my back pulls again as I swing my arms. I ignore it.

"A child's bedroom set," Laura murmurs. "A wheelchair. Building supplies."

I slow down. "That doesn't make any sense."

"I know," Laura says quietly. "But there it is."

"You think our thief's stealing to support his family?" John sounds dubious.

"Not to the tune of over a billion dollars," I drawl. But now I'm intrigued. "Keep digging," I instruct Laura. "I want to know as much as possible on how this money is being spent."

"I'll devote all my time to it," she promises.

"Wait a second. Brick and mortar. You say our thief is going to local stores to buy big ticket items? They have to be delivered somewhere, don't they?" John sounds excited suddenly.

"That is true," Laura muses. "I'll get that information, and I'll see if I can find any security footage from the times of purchase. If none of the recipients have any leads back to our hacker, maybe we can catch their face on camera."

It's definite progress. Feeling optimistic, I open my mouth to give the go-ahead—just as my phone beeps at me. Someone has sent an e-mail to my work account. "Okay, do it," I say distractedly, bringing up my mail app.

Then I pause for a long time, staring at my phone, my legs swinging to a stop. It's from an unfamiliar e-mail address—obviously a throwaway. I open it and blink several times as I read the few lines.

"I'll call you as soon as we have something more," Laura is promising, but I barely hear her.

"Of course," I manage, and the call disconnects as I read the anonymous e-mail again.

Dr. Yoshida did not steal from you. Do not confront him.

Don Rocco Marcone thinks that you stole from him. Be careful.

You were targeted by mistake.

Is this a leak from one of my thief's associates, or an attack of conscience by the thief himself? I start working out again, my mind racing as I mull over how—and if—I should answer the strange message.

CHAPTER 5

Robin

Only once the warning is out to Drake Steele can I finally sleep. I don't feel relief as I drift off, only a sort of deep resignation. I may very well have just signed my death warrant—literally dying by my principles. At least I'll die with a clean conscience.

The rain taps against the thin wood barely two inches from the top of my head. The refrigerator crate I found in the alley has leaks; I've lined it with cardboard, but that's starting to get soaked through.

I hide inside, balled up and shivering, praying that none of the drunks will find me before I can steal a few hours of sleep. They had good fun chasing me down the alley a couple of nights ago. I don't think I can handle another scare like that any time soon.

I'm twelve, but I feel half my age. I'm terrified, curled into a ball, choking down sobs so no one will hear me over the rain. Don't let them find me, *I pray. I already have finger-bruises under my jeans from where one of them grabbed my hip.*

I want my Mom. I want my Dad. I want my old home back, and my books, and my bed.

I don't want this icy winter, this city turned ugly and dark, its men turned into monsters.

A drop of rain works its way through the cardboard and strikes me in the head like a small, icy rock. I bury my face in my hands and wonder again why there's no one to help.

The ping of an e-mail alert drags me out of the cardboard box and back into my warm apartment. I lift my head groggily, brain full of fuzz, tears still drying on my cheeks.

I promised myself that I would never let anyone else go through what I had, not so long as I could do something about it.

It's full morning. Rain's tapping on the window, and I nod grimly, knowing now what evoked that old memory. I'm not angry; rain means it's above freezing again.

For once, I'm reluctant to crawl out of bed and scrape myself together to get back to work at my desk. I haven't slept enough. I've been through hell, and I don't know when I'll be able to get myself back to sleep again if I get up now.

I squint my eyes against the thin sunlight, pulling deeper under the covers. Whatever the message is, it can wait.

I'm still lying there with my eyes open several minutes later, and I finally sigh and get up. "Damn it." The loneliness from the dream, the fear and despair, are still nibbling on the bottom of my heart as I head for the bathroom. *Maybe I should get a pet or something.*

After showering and dressing in black jeans and a gray wool sweater, I force myself to eat something before my trip back into cyberspace. I'll need a walk eventually, some kind of real exercise. On top of everything else going on, I'm starting to feel cooped up.

For now, a couple of hardboiled eggs, a bowl of quick oatmeal with apple slices, and a banana will have to do. I swallow my usual fistful of vitamins and supplements before cleaning up my tiny kitchen and heading over to see what's going on online.

I open the window that pinged me—and freeze.

Oh no. No, no, no. What is he doing? I should have just closed the damned e-mail account an hour after I sent the message!

Drake Steele just wrote me back unexpectedly, and for a solid minute I just stare at the message indicator without opening it. Then I close my eyes and click on it.

I have to force them open, and I force them to look at my screen.

Thank you for the warning. I can only guess that you had an attack of conscience.

I would like my money back, and I would like an explanation.

I can't catch my breath. My ears are ringing suddenly with my earlier warning to myself. *Do not interact.*

It's too dangerous...but on the other hand, if I just robbed someone who's relatively innocent, he at least deserves an explanation. Doesn't he?

I send him back a short note, knowing that the mail server I'm using can't be traced back to me. The whole time, I feel tugged in two different directions. And yet somehow, though it takes me twenty minutes to write and send a few short lines, I feel better for sending it.

That money is pocket change to a man like you, but I'm going to use it to save seven thousand lives.

I just don't want you dying because of all this. The other two might deserve it, but I have my doubts about you now.

I sit back, closing my eyes. Suddenly the walls of the apartment seem to be squeezing together around me. I need to get out of here, rain or not.

My boot heels clack on the wet sidewalk as I walk up the

street toward the closest corner shop, four blocks away. After the icy cold and snow, Seattle's version of a January thaw has filled the air with swirling mist. I pass the burned-out building, turning my face away from it, my head throbbing with my failure.

At least the survivors will have enough money to start their lives over. But nothing I do will feel like enough. Not after we lost five lives.

I try to block those thoughts and think of Drake Steele instead. I can't get him out of my head—his good looks, his self-assurance, how fast he caught on to who sent him that message, his audacity in writing me back and expecting an answer.

And then I went and gave him one, just like he wanted. *What the hell is wrong with me?* This man is dangerous; I can feel it in my bones. He's already gotten me to do things against my better judgment.

He's trouble. He'd be trouble even if he didn't mean to be. Why is he having this much of an effect on me?

I'm actually getting a little scared now, the fear seeping past my exhausted resignation. *Whatever happens, I have to stay focused on helping those people. Nothing is more important than that.*

The corner store shares the first floor of a nice old building with a coffee shop on one side and a used book shop on the other. Inside is a typical Seattle compromise: one wall full of produce and healthy snacks, the other wall full of salt, sugar, and grease.

The chubby little Persian guy behind the counter is listening patiently to a customer's request for more varieties of tofu. He gives me a resigned little smile, and we nod at each other as I walk in. He sees me every couple of days and always seems a little relieved at the sight of a customer who won't twitter odd requests at him in too-rapid English.

I get a big bottle of premixed nutritional shake, a thick organic glop of an unpleasant mossy color thanks to lots of spirulina. I know I don't eat or sleep enough, so hopefully choices like this will help make up the difference.

I pay the cashier in exact change, and he smiles as we exchange well-wishes, and I walk back out. I think he believes I'm much younger than I am. He's asked me more than once where my mother is.

I think he'd cringe if I told him the truth.

My body must crave something in the shake, because the smell when I open it has me gulping it down greedily even as I make my way back down the street. *If Drake wants his money back, then he can go directly and ask for it back from each person I've helped—and preferably face-to-face.*

But even though I talk tough in my head as I march back to my apartment, my resolve crumbles when I sit down at my screen and see he's written back. Again.

You fascinate me. If you tell me about these seven thousand people you're saving with my money, I'll let you keep it all with no further trouble.

There's just one catch. I want to hear it from you in person —and I want you to bring some form of documentation on these guerrilla charity acts of yours that I can verify.

I push away from my desk so suddenly that I almost knock my chair over. "Oh no. No, no, no, no, that is a bad idea." And probably a trap.

I write him back.

I'll give you all pertinent details on how the money was used, but I don't meet. It's a matter of personal safety.

I switch windows resolutely and force myself to go back to solving people's problems with that stolen money. Candace Whitman: hospital bills, $48,000. The Rodriguez family: overdue mortgage, $40,000.

Purple Heart recipient Aisha Michaels: vet bills for her

service dog, changes to her house to accommodate her new disabilities, $37,000.

It only takes an average year's pay to change someone's life forever. *Anyone who says that money can't buy happiness has never known the misery of not having enough.*

I'm ten families into the day's "customers" when I hear the beep of a reply e-mail. I stop, and my heart starts to pound again. "Shit."

Knock it off, Steele! I'm not meeting with you! I switch windows—and my eyes widen in horror.

He's sent a photo attachment. It's me.

Blurry footage of my hair tucked under my hat and my body wrapped in a fuzzy gray coat that isn't my style at all—it's one of my disguises. The image is taken from a big-box store where I handled some of my furniture orders for my "clients" early yesterday.

He must have broken into their security system and stolen this image. No way would he be able to get the information this fast any other way—not even bribery.

I know you're in Seattle. I know you're making cold-wallet Bitcoin purchases with my money and sending them to individuals and families throughout the city. I'm assuming they are part of your seven thousand.

I sit very still, just staring at the screen. *How did he find me so fast?*

A chat message pops up with another photo—it's me again, and this time, it's very clear. Cute little me from almost a decade ago—innocent, smiling, well-dressed, and very blonde.

You were a cute kid, Miss Locke. I'm sure you're lovely now, and I suspect that you have noble aims. But you're not walking off with a third of a billion of my money without a face-to-face.

I sit there shivering in a mix of anger, embarrassment, and

fear as he gives me an address and a time. It's an upscale bar and grill downtown.

Tonight. It's nice and public. You'll be quite safe. But if you don't show up, I will find you.

How...? I think numbly, and then I sit back and close my eyes. *He's got me.*

I'll see you there.

Guess I'm going to dinner.

CHAPTER 6

Drake

"All right. I don't want to go to this meeting blind. I want every single detail you've dug up on Robin Locke, and I mean everything. I don't care how boring or trivial it seems." I look at Laura as she sits across the desk from me, and she nods, typing a few commands into her laptop.

"I'll send you the compilation I have right now and then anything else I find before eight this evening. Are you sure about meeting this woman?" Laura looks back up at me worriedly.

I let out a hearty laugh. "I'm really not that worried, Laura," I reassure. "I'll be armed, John will be in shouting distance, and from what you have been able to pick up so far, our hacker is a loner, or has been since Spider's Web went down."

Laura nods and lets out a soft sigh. "I just don't entirely trust these anarchistic types. You never really know what a hacker is going to do. Or why."

I sit back in my desk chair and check my computer for her forwarded files, opening them one by one.

Robin Locke, age 24, Americanized British citizen. Born in Washington, D.C. on March 8, 1994 to a British diplomat and his wife. Parents died in a car accident when she was twelve. Custody was granted to Wentworth Locke, her paternal uncle, and all property was transferred into his name.

"So why wasn't she brought back to Britain? Or did her uncle come here?"

"Briefly," Laura replies, and there's such a strangely grim tone to her voice that I immediately start reading again. She's filled in the notes with more information as she collects it. There's a lot more detail now.

Wentworth Locke sold all US properties held by the family, liquidated all assets and took a private plane back to London three months after his brother's death. It was presumed that Robin went with him. But Robin's paperwork for British repatriation was never submitted, she was never admitted to school, and she has no medical records in Britain.

My eyes widen. This part is new, and it makes our little anarchist's rage make sudden, terrible sense. "Am I reading here that the man left her behind on the streets?"

"There's little if any evidence that she spent any time in London. That winter, she was admitted to D.C.'s public hospital with severe pneumonia, malnutrition, and exposure." Laura winces as she sees my face.

"He robbed her. He robbed her and dumped her." I blink slowly, staring at the lines of text in front of me. *Riches to rags...a talented young girl from a wealthy family, dumped and pretty much left to die. No wonder she has a vendetta against the rich.*

And that has me wondering about her pledge to save thousands of lives with her stolen money. She likes movies, apparently. *A Fistful of Dollars, Robin Hood.* Of course, the second one would stick with her, given the name her parents gave her.

And of course, after what she's been through, that story's morals would have stuck, too.

"Every last one of the donations we traced went to a family or individual facing homelessness or destitution, right?" I ask thoughtfully.

"That's right. If she disposed of the rest the same way, she's basically practicing some kind of...guerrilla charity." Laura sounds baffled, but I just smile, because that's exactly what it is.

My little movie buff. Steal from the rich, give to the poor.

It's starting to get hard to stay mad at her. I'm still planning to turn this situation to my advantage, but...perhaps she can be part of that—in a non-antagonistic way.

Of course, if she decides to screw me over further instead, I'll have to destroy her. But I really hope it doesn't come to that.

"Any further hospitalizations, applications for benefits, anything?" I keep skimming forward through the text, but I'm not finding much. "There's a gap here of about ten years."

Laura looks up from her screen. "We're suspecting that she erased some of her own history. Maybe a juvenile criminal record, maybe a foster parent she doesn't want connected to her...I'm really not sure."

Locke was briefly under investigation as part of an underground Seattle hacking ring known as Spider's Web. It was disbanded in 2011 after the ringleader was accidentally killed in a police raid.

This part I've read through already, but the addendum beneath surprises me and makes me smirk at the same time.

Almost immediately after the raid, the Nudes Exchange scandal struck Seattle PD leading to the discipline of over a dozen officers. That was followed by the release of several

suppressed and very incriminating dashcam tapes resulting in four officers being fired, two jailed. This was followed by...

"Wow. So, she was behind the Great SPD Shitstorm of 2011. She must have really loved this Spider guy. Maybe he and his friends took her in off the streets?"

"Maybe so." Laura taps her lower lip with the tip of her stylus. "If she had the skill to do these sorts of hacks seven years ago, I feel a little better about her slipping past all our security." She looks at me and then blushes. "I'm sorry. I shouldn't—"

"No, you're right. The kid's a rock star when it comes to hacking. But what she doesn't have is a team, like you, me, and the IT boys. Apparently, she is pretty used to being part of one. I'm wondering if she misses it." I scratch my chin, scrolling down further. "No current, clear photos of her?"

"There isn't a single current image of her anywhere online except for what we pulled off those security camera images. And even with enhancements, she was covering her hair and eyes. Only the facial recognition AI was able to get a lock on her, and even then, I had to expand the age parameters before I got a real hit."

"Alright, have the AI spit out an aged-up image of those photos of her at twelve. I want some clue of who I'm looking for when I walk into that restaurant. Otherwise, I'm at a real disadvantage."

I scroll to the bottom. Robin Locke has been slowly building a small fortune in real estate purchases in South Park. All low-income housing, all fixed up to well above industry standards since she bought them, all just barely making enough profit to continue improvements.

I check the files on the buildings owned by Greenhood Properties, her sole proprietorship. *Look at these.* LEED certifications, solar and wind installations, building battery banks, emergency generators, insulation ratings so high you could be cozy in a

Boston winter. Five-year leases with no rent raises. *She isn't profiting off these tenants, she's protecting them.*

Laura is typing away as I mull over the documents. "Done. Just give it a few moments. I need to ask—what are you planning to do once you've made contact?" She sounds a little concerned.

I look up at her, the last of my anger having ebbed away somewhere between learning about Miss Locke's past and looking over those building improvements. "She's made a mess. She needs to work with us to clean it up. If she's cooperative, performs well, and can sufficiently justify this 'noble cause' she robbed me for, I'll want to take advantage of her strengths. Once the danger of having gangsters banging down my door has passed, I'm giving serious thought to offering her a place on our team."

She tenses slightly. "IT?" She's still blaming herself for the breach and is clearly worried about being replaced because of her failure. It's an industry standard for the IT head to take the fall for a breach. But I don't operate that way, and we designed those systems together. I'm just as much at fault as her.

"No, actually, charitable giving." At her surprised look, I flash a grin. "If she's not just some ass who's fortifying her conscience with a little financial kindness, if this really is her mission..."

I pause, considering the documents in front of me. My anger at this woman's invasion of my life has been replaced by fascination and deep curiosity. Perhaps it is because I understand something of the lonely terror and helpless rage that her younger self must have felt—the same that I once felt as a young boy before I got stronger.

Robin's also right. Those twenty-five thousand Bitcoins were chump change for me. My investments alone will make that money back for me in less than six months.

It all hinges on what happens when we meet. But I'll give her a chance. One chance.

I chuckle with a bravado I don't entirely feel. "If she's so keen on spending my money saving people's lives and homes, maybe I'll keep her busy doing just that."

Laura actually smiles a little; I know she's struggling to hide her relief. "Well, keeping her busy would keep her out of trouble."

"Maybe. She does seem to have an awful lot of energy." And drive.

This is the kind of person who takes out their anger at the world by making it a better place. I don't particularly appreciate being caught up in that fury, but if Robin Locke ends up adding her considerable talents to my team as a result, I'll take it.

Another message notice arrives: the AI has finished its work. I open the results.

Well, damn.

Robin Locke is beautiful. Even with the awkward, doll-like smoothness of a simulated likeness, she looks like a sweet-faced, delicate, blonde angel with enormous brown eyes. I look at her, and I want to hide her away from the cold of the world, and then...well.

It's been a while since I've had a woman in my bed. I've been too busy. But it doesn't mean I don't miss it. Looking at her image, I suddenly remember how much.

"Very good," I say distractedly. "I'm going to get ready. If you find anything else, make sure I have it before I get on the road."

"Of course." Laura bends back over her laptop as I get up to go take a shower.

At eight sharp I'm sitting at one of my restaurants downtown, pre-gaming with a single Manhattan, which I nurse very slowly as I watch the door. The walls are made of structural-strength glass panels, thick enough that the rain striking their outsides is distorted a little. From my seat at the edge of the mezzanine above the bar, I can covertly watch everyone walking or driving by outside.

The door opens one minute after eight, and a slight figure strides in, wrapped in fawn-colored gabardine. She puts her hood down, and I blink slightly as I focus on her face and the glossy mane of shoulder-length hair surrounding it.

The AI had the face nailed. She has the innocent features of a Renaissance angel. She hasn't gone heavy on the makeup—it's all tasteful and subtle...except for short fingernails the color of steel—and that hair.

She looks like a class act, too, in all aspects but one. Those tresses. Soft flattering waves, dyed in multiple colors, giving it depth and texture...but...those colors are all shades of green. Emerald strands shimmer in the light as she shakes out her hair and takes off her coat, revealing an aubergine dress and tights beneath. A simple strand of steel-colored pearls crosses her throat. She looks like a punk—an elegant punk, tastefully outrageous.

I wonder if she has any tattoos under that dress. And then I have to fight down a surge of lusty curiosity, because apparently my cock doesn't give a damn what color her hair is.

I stand after a moment, ignoring any mild awkwardness, and gesture to the hostess. She nods and goes to bring Miss Locke up to me.

"Good evening," I greet the young hacker once the hostess has left us alone on the mezzanine. "Thank you for joining me, Miss Locke."

CHAPTER 7

Robin

He's even hotter in person. Big, graceful, the faint scent of an expensive, spicy cologne hanging around him. Photos can't capture the power of those steely eyes or the subtle play of emotions across his beautiful face.

I could watch him all day. *That's dangerous.*

He pulls out my chair for me as I try to figure out how to respond. "Thank you," I finally manage as I sit down. "Not like you gave me much choice."

"I apologize for that. But even though you may have included me in your little... venture...by mistake, actions have consequences, and this needs to be put right." He smiles tightly as he settles into his chair, his eyes locked with mine.

I stare back, resolving not to let him take full control of the conversation. Rich guys always act like they have the right to dominate those around them. It pisses me off.

"I'll help get Marcone off your tail," I say quickly in a low voice. "And if you want to know how the money was spent, I'll show you. But I swear to God, if you go after those people I'm helping—"

He holds up a hand, sounding tired but firm. "I'm not going to go after them. I just want to know what task is so important that you would risk making such dangerous enemies to complete it."

I pause, sizing him up again. Past all that self-assured, dominant beauty, the man across the table from me doesn't actually seem angry. Not unhappy at all, actually. Instead, he seems very curious.

I hesitate on the edge of opening up a little, skittish as a stray cat with this stranger who has every reason to want to ruin my life. "So, you didn't bring the police. I'm presuming you didn't bring recording equipment, since that fan up there puts out enough white noise to ruin any attempt."

"That's deliberate," he replies smoothly. "I'm not here to call the police on you, lead you into a trap, or gather incriminating evidence. I want exactly what I asked for. The truth."

He's being a gentleman about this, way more than I probably deserve at this point, especially from his point of view. I lay my briefcase on the table, open it, and pull out a folder of printouts.

"Last night alone your money saved these families from everything from foreclosure to death. If you want me to apologize for that, I'm not going to. But if you want me to apologize for mistaking you for someone you're not, and for potentially getting you in trouble with those...other guys, I'll kiss your fucking boot."

His eyebrows climb toward his hairline. But then he just smiles lopsidedly and rumbles, "That won't be necessary. But given your vehement free-spiritedness, I'll take the apology with the gravity you intended."

"Good. If I didn't feel like crap about catching you up in

this, we wouldn't be talking." I slide the folders over to him. I've redacted all contact information and social security numbers—he could probably still find them, but it won't be by my hand.

"The whole idea is to make those who don't give a damn pay their share anyway and save people who don't have a chance otherwise. But you're already paying yours. I should have caught that."

I can't stand sloppy work. I know that the mess with the apartment next door knocked my emotions off the rails and is half to blame for my rash decision, but it's more than that. I was just looking for rich guys who ticked enough boxes on my "evil" list to justify stealing from. *Hell, I vetted my recipients more closely than I did my "donors."*

"You're blushing," he comments without looking up from the profiles he's slowly paging through. There is the tiniest note of teasing in his voice.

"I...uh...ah..." *Shit!* How does he do that, without even really trying?

I'm blushing even harder now, and I can't stop. I stare down at the tabletop, my face burning. "Look, I'm just bothered that this happened. Let's not make a big deal over some dilated capillaries."

"Oh, I'm not, but apparently you are." His lips curve in a faint, lopsided smile before he goes back to reading. "Why not pick targets halfway across the world, or give to people well away from where you are, to keep anyone from connecting you to this location?"

It's a fair question. I can't tell him how little I actually care about my own outcome in this, as long as I finish the job, so instead I simply say, "This is my community. And their needs are more important than my safety."

"And so, apparently, is my safety," he murmurs, sounding

even more intrigued. "You're poised to die for your ideals, aren't you? Rather than risk an innocent man getting killed?"

I snort. "Yes, except for one thing—you're not any more innocent than I am."

"Actually, I'm probably significantly less so," he admits calmly. "But that is not who I wish to be any more."

I gaze into his eyes and feel something in me untether and drift toward him, like a riptide pulling me far out into a warm sea. My heart aches with a longing I don't fully understand, and I realize too late that he's more dangerous than I ever anticipated.

"Me neither," I whisper breathlessly, looking everywhere but at him.

"How did you choose the recipients?" he asks calmly, voice gone smooth and businesslike again. It helps. I focus back on the conversation, which he's approaching in the manner of a man who is about to close a business deal.

"I crawled social media, local listings of foreclosures in progress, registries with collection agencies. Things like that." I'm playing it casual. The same data collection AI I coded to gather dirt on Washington's billionaires also sniffed out the suffering and at-risk among the locals with little effort.

In fact, narrowing the number of recipients down to twenty thousand had left me with a lingering stomachache for weeks. It was like doing triage in a trauma hospital. "Basically, I picked people who would be completely sunk if I didn't step in."

He tilts his head just slightly. "There's one thing I don't understand. Your parents were quite wealthy. Why didn't you steal your inheritance back from your uncle?"

The shock of him mentioning my past pulls a bitter laugh from my throat before I can stop it. For one terrible moment, I'm back watching the strange man in the dark suit lock the gate of my home. *I ask him where my uncle is as I clutch my one suitcase to* me, and he says, "I'm sure I don't know," before he walks off, leaving me there.

"If you're going to invade my privacy in return, I'll ask you to at least get the facts straight." Briefly, my face is down in my hands. But I manage to raise my head with all the strength of will I can spare.

He's watching me, his brows drawn together—a look of sympathetic concern on his face that shocks me. "Why don't you tell me what happened, then?"

"He has friends and connections at Interpol and the Yard, even the FBI. I have only ever been able to take back little bits of what is mine and make his online life very inconvenient. I've never really been able to avenge myself." I rub my face, not wanting him to see the threatening tears.

You don't show weakness. If you do, people pounce. I berate myself internally until I can compose myself.

"I'm assuming you've at least gotten some form of poetic revenge?" he asks a bit urgently, just a little edge of anger to his tone.

I stare at him. That makes it even worse. The man is *empathizing*. Or he's putting on such a good act that I can't tell the difference. The former is unimaginable. The latter frightens me so much I can only hope it isn't true.

"What do you care?" I challenge in a low, pointed voice.

He seems to snap out of some kind of reverie, and his smile becomes wry. "I guess that was a touch personal. I just don't like the idea of the bastard getting away with it."

"Oh, he isn't getting away with it. He's just not aware of that." I don't divulge the details, and that only seems to intrigue him further.

It's true, though. In the last five years, my uncle's wife left him over gambling debts that didn't exist, he lost any chance at a political life after his abandonment of me became very public, and he doesn't know at all where some of his money is disappearing to. He's developed a drinking problem, which makes it even harder to keep track of things.

And yet of course, it's not enough. It's never enough.

"So, this is what you do. You set the rich and wicked against each other or punish them individually, siphoning off their money, and keep those who have no chance otherwise from falling completely into the dark." His tone is too warm.

My heart starts pounding. I look out the glass wall at the traffic splashing past and swallow hard. "There's a certain emptiness that you feel when you realize that no one in the world gives a damn about you or what happens to you, and that most of the people who could do something about it are only out for themselves."

He speaks up in a low, solemn tone—and all but finishes my thought as I slowly turn my gaze back to him. "Suddenly you must live or die by your own strength and wits, and maybe any allies you can make along the way. You must learn to be tough, even if you're terrified. And the whole time, the one scrap of humanity that you manage to hold onto—your conscience, your principles—pains you daily and may one day will get you killed."

I swallow, my mouth painfully dry. "How do you know that?"

"I lived it, too." Now it's his turn to look away, and I realize he's got his own reservations about trusting me, though he's trying to reach past them.

Or he could be playing me for a fool. I have no way of knowing. I can only trust him...or not. "Is that why you are more interested in finding out how the money's being used than...revenge?"

"That's part of it. The other part is that since we're apparently going to be working together for a bit to rectify this situation, I want to see how you handle your 'rescues.'" He's turned back into the smooth businessman again, and I'm both relieved and disappointed.

"What's your interest?" I'm suddenly uncertain where he's going with this. He keeps surprising me; I'm not sure whether I like it or not.

I just wish I didn't feel warm all over every time his lips curve into a smile.

"I want you," he says, and the three words ring right through me, sending a jolt down to the pit of my stomach.

What?

He goes on in an amused tone. "I do a lot of my own charity work—quietly, so I'm not constantly being hit up for donations. I wouldn't condone breaking into people's bank accounts so that you can settle their financial affairs for them, but I have to admit, I'm impressed with your work thus far."

Impressed? I'm still wary. I'm not used to being flattered, and my cheeks are prickling again. "Why?"

"You're organized and thorough. Maybe not thorough enough, or else we wouldn't be here, but I suspect that that's a direct result of constantly biting off more than you can chew." He holds up the sheaf of printouts. "Your plan is ambitious, but I doubt you can accomplish it all alone in anything like a timely manner."

I hitch in a breath. "I'm prepared to put in as long as it takes."

"Yes, and I'm sure you're quick as well as thorough. However, even if you spend as little as twenty minutes on each family or individual, you can't clear more than a dozen or so people an hour. That's a hundred and twenty people in a ten-hour shift. How many people are on your list?"

Trust him. For now. "Twenty thousand."

He lets out a low whistle. "That will take you one hundred and sixty-seven days to complete, if you work every day. You say that these people need help *now*. I would like to make you a deal."

"What deal?" I don't know if my alarms are ringing more because he's expecting so much trust from me, or because I suddenly want to give it so very badly.

I've ached for someone out there, a man especially, to understand me—*truly* understand me, the way Spider and the boys did before the cops scattered my makeshift hacker family to the winds. I've dreamed about it for a long time. I've just never gone after it, because what do I even know anymore about any kind of real interactions outside of cyberspace?

But suddenly, here is this stunningly gorgeous man that I shouldn't trust at all, yet who seems to understand me so much.

The hostess comes up to check on us, and Drake looks up at her. "Menus in five minutes," he instructs, and she nods and withdraws.

He turns back to me. "I enjoy personally intervening in the lives of needy people, in a way similar to your own, which is why I've been quietly sponsoring people on donation sites for years. But as satisfying as it is, I face a similar dilemma to your own. There isn't enough time in the day to help all the people that I'd like to."

My eyebrows rise. "So...what? We work together to get this done?"

"Yes." He leans toward me across the table, his eyes gleaming. "I want in on what you're doing. I want to participate. A third of this is coming from my money, after all, and if you agree to my deal, it will be my money exclusively that you'll be distributing from now on."

I'm staring at him again. I blink and look away. "I'm not following."

"Once things are settled here, and this...incident...is behind us, I want you to work for me on an exclusive contract of at least three years. I'll give you a budget, a space, and a team to work under you. We'll get your twenty thousand what they need, and then help an additional ten thousand people a year."

He can't be serious!

But...what if he is? I take a shivery breath and look down. "Can I think about this?"

"Of course. However, the offer will be off the table in forty-eight hours." His voice is warm and firm, and for a moment, caught in my storm of emotions, my eyes fix on the curve of his lips as he speaks.

I catch myself wondering what they would feel like on my skin, and gasp slightly, looking away. "Of course."

We both order steak and dark beer and talk more lightly around bites of our meal. "So, why green?" he asks me. "It's eye-catching and well-kept, but it's not exactly inconspicuous."

I wince slightly, but he's smiling kindly at me with no judgment in his eyes. My stomach tightens...and then I relax my guard a bit more. "My natural hair color is too close to my uncle's," I say simply. "And I wanted to make a statement."

"What sort of statement?" His eyes narrow with amusement, that teasing smile making me squeeze my knees together under the table. "You look like a punk. A sexy, well-dressed punk."

"I am a punk," I reply with a touch of defiance. "I'm a cyberpunk. But it doesn't mean I can't have taste." I toss my head defiantly—and then notice something that makes my heart beat even faster.

His eyes follow the sweep of my hair as it bounces across my shoulders and then settles down again, and I see a gleam enter them like a tiny ember. "And you do," he murmurs, voice lowering to a purr. "Beauty, as well."

I look away, cheeks burning again, and feel panic well up inside me. *He has me wrapped around his finger. Yesterday, he was a target. Now he's talking like he wants to hire me—or fuck me. Maybe both.*

Having a man call me beautiful and sexy is nothing new. It happens any time I run into guys in bars, clubs, or in the street—guys who are looking for Miss Right Now and don't feel like paying a price other than a cheap compliment. But this...this is different. I feel it down to my toes.

Maybe his idea of revenge is to seduce me with promises of money, sex, and affection, only to drop me on my ass like my uncle once did. Drake is observant enough to know how much that would hurt.

Or maybe he's one of those guys who can lust after you with everything he has, while planning the whole time to slip a knife in your back.

Or maybe he's sincere. Somehow, that possibility frightens me the most out of all of them. Because I have no defense against sincerity. I barely know what it looks like any more. Not since Spider died.

"Don't do that. That's not fair," I mumble uncomfortably and busy myself with another big bite of steak. I suddenly worry that I may not have much more time left for my meal. Will I have to get out of here? My heart's pounding again.

"I'm sorry? What isn't?" he asks in such an innocent tone that it hurts.

"Don't hit on me." My hands are shaking. I hide them on my knees.

He scoffs in surprise. "Why not? Are you involved with someone?"

"I know you're just trying to put me off my guard, so I'll do what you want. There's no need. Just be direct with me, and don't...do that." I take a few deep breaths.

"Is that what you think I'm doing?" He has an incredulous laugh in his voice, but one look in my eyes, and he hesitates.

"Oh. I see it is. I'm sorry for any confusion I've caused, but... that's not what I'm about."

"What are you about, then?" I'm still not following.

"It's simple. If you're capable of doing as good a job as I think you'll do, then I want you on my team. That part, however, is separate from noticing just how attractive and charming you are."

He winks, and I feel my breath freeze in my chest as my toes curl. "Oh," I mumble, and go back to eating mechanically.

Oh God. Oh crap. What do I do?

He watches me for a while, looking even more intrigued than before. "You don't really date, do you?" he asks finally, and I shake my head.

"No time." *No experience. No trust, either.*

"So, you're not used to men being attracted to you." He's gazing at me steadily again.

"Not unless they want to take advantage. You...you have every reason to want revenge on me. I'm still getting used to the idea that you might actually...support what I'm doing. That you're not about to f—"

His grin flashes and I stop short. Because I have a feeling that he'd happily fuck me if I brought it up, but that...wasn't exactly what I was talking about.

"I don't really care what happens to me from all this," I admit. "But I just don't want it to happen before I finish my work. So, I have to be careful. In...*all* ways."

"I see." He still seems amused, and not put off in the least. He simply sits back and says, "All right then. How about you sleep on my offer, and I'll have a look into your work with these...clients. We'll talk tomorrow."

I nod slowly, picking at my meal. "That's fair." I wonder, however, if his other...proposal...the implied one that shocked me just as much as the first did, is going to get revisited as well.

The very thought makes me realize that I'm going to get a lot of work done tonight...because the thought of him wanting me *like that* is going to keep me awake for a whole new reason.

Is he toying with me? Can I trust him? His smile is impenetrable, and yet I get the feeling that those eyes can see right through me. Right down to the girl huddled in the cardboard box who is still praying that no man will hurt her again.

CHAPTER 8

Drake

For once, nightmares don't greet me when I fall asleep. Instead, I'm tumbling back and forth on my bed in the dark, totally wrapped up in the woman in my arms.

We're frenzied with need for each other, gasping for air, our limbs tangling together. She whimpers and strains against me as I part her thighs, her hips lifting in slow circles as she offers herself.

"Don't stop," she whispers in my ear as she clings to me. I thrust into her and sensation travels through my body, hazy pleasure rising past my hips. She moans, nails stinging my shoulders as I ride her closer and closer to the edge of ecstasy.

In the dream, her head falls back as she climaxes, and I see that silky mop of emerald-colored hair for just a moment before my own body takes off.

I shout myself awake in the dim room, thrashing free of my blankets, my hips pushing upward against nothing. My voice echoes off the walls, and I realize that I am alone. The climax leaves me shuddering with pleasure even as the disappointment hits.

I collapse back to my mattress, sticky and tingling, yet still unfulfilled. I lie there panting for a moment, knowing I need a damn shower but still longing for the woman in my dream. The one who wronged me, the one I just met...the one I can't stop thinking about.

Robin. *Holy shit this woman is trouble,* I think, a moment before I push past my haze and shove myself out of my bed.

But I like her kind of trouble.

I'm in the shower when my phone starts ringing. I finish rinsing off, wrap a robe around myself, and wander out, yawning, to see who it is. The phone keeps ringing until I pick it up. "It's four thirty in the morning."

"Yes, sir." It's one of the desk guards, and he sounds pretty damned nervous. "I'm sorry for the intrusion, sir, but there are two very large Italian men in suits down here."

I blink slowly. *Shit. Here we go.* "All right. Let them up. Do not escort them, and let John know we have a Scenario Six as soon as the elevator doors close behind them."

"Yes, sir." He hangs up. Sighing, I get dressed in a good black suit and make sure I have my Beretta handy.

Five minutes later, the door slides open, and two of Don Rocco's enforcers come in. I would know them at once for what they are from both their enormous size and the way their shoulder holsters show against the jackets of their ill-fitting suits. They pause as they come in, and the larger, older one narrows his small eyes as he looks me over, clearly not expecting to find me sitting calmly alone behind my loft desk.

"Help you gentlemen with something?" I ask quietly as I stand. The pistol gleams next to my keyboard—I've made sure they can't see it from their angle.

They look at each other and then walk up to my desk and stand over it, arms folded. I sit back down as they approach, sliding the pistol into my lap. Neither seems to notice. The smaller one, who has a scar cutting into his jowl on one side, steps forward and speaks.

"We're here as representatives of Mr. Marcone. I'm sure you're familiar." They sound overly casual; they seem to have forgotten that they're in a highly secured building and have only gotten this far because I allowed it.

"I am. But Mr. Marcone and I don't have any business dealings, so I'm confused as to why he arranged this sudden early morning visit." I play innocent, just as calm and casual as they.

"Oh, I think you know," comes the almost sarcastic reply, and I do my best not to bristle. So much ego in these men—and so little competence to back it up.

"Look," I say, gesturing toward the small wet bar I keep by my desk. "Let's pretend for a moment that it's well before dawn, I haven't had sufficient sleep or coffee, and your boss and I have never had a problem before. Oh wait, that's the absolute truth. So please, excuse me if I'm hazy about where I stepped on your esteemed boss's toes."

"He had a bunch of that Bitcoin stuff stolen from him," sighs Scarface. He jerks his head at the bruiser, who goes to fill two tumblers halfway with eighty-year old Scotch. "Our IT guy traced them to your account."

I blink, and then—after making sure the pistol is concealed on my lap—open my laptop and bring up the affected Bitcoin accounts. I am going to be partially transparent at this point...partially. If I'm going to put up a smokescreen, it's going to be so close to the truth that only Robin will be concealed by it.

Robin. I'm not sure why I'm protecting her, especially since I know that Marcone is looking for a convenient fall guy. Except that she and I are so alike in so many painful little ways...and she doesn't actually deserve this.

I don't imagine that she's gotten much in her life that she actually does deserve. But maybe I can help change that.

Bottom line: I like her. I want her talents at my disposal and her dainty little green-haired self in my bed. And none of that is going to happen if I let Marcone have her. "I want to show you some information from my Bitcoin accounts from four days ago. This is confidential information, so please don't let it go any further than your employer."

"Of course." They seem confused that I'm treating this with the calm, respectful formality of a business transaction. Maybe even relieved. Both men crowd in behind me, and after setting up a redacting program to scramble my sensitive information, I show the window in question.

"At a little later than this time four days ago, I received an alert from my IT team that my own accounts had been robbed. But right before they were robbed, I got a transfer of Bitcoin from an unknown source. That money was then transferred out of my account within the hour, along with another twenty-five thousand Bitcoin of my own."

I show them the transactions. The big one grunts and looks at his senior. "The numbers match what the Boss said he lost," he rasps.

"So, someone sticks a bunch of our money in your account, and then pulls that and some money of yours out and sends it somewhere else. Do you know where?" They go back to their seats, and I feel myself relax slightly. They didn't notice the gun.

I hesitate for a split second, realizing that they'll notice if I take too long. *They'll trace the other transaction to Yoshida no matter what I do. But I will not be the one to implicate him—one undeserved enemy is more than enough.* "We're still determining where the money went from there. But your boss and I could both simply be links in a chain of such transactions."

"So, whoever this is robbed a bunch of people at once, shuffling money through their accounts as he went?" Scarface is smart. Maybe too smart. *Handle him carefully.*

"Well, if my theory is correct, then yes."

The big one frowns. "The Boss wants his money and the hand of whoever did this to him. But if this is a frame-up, we'd be bringing him the wrong hand and the real thief will get off free."

"Look, gentlemen," I say calmly as I watch the two idiots drink down my good Scotch like water. In this rainstorm, they're probably going to end up totaling their car if they keep drinking like this. But I'm not here to keep goons from dying of stupidity.

"Besides what I've just shown you, I have the two best reasons in the world to not be your thief. The first part is that I do not want or need Mr. Rocco's money. The second is that I certainly don't want or need Mr. Rocco as an enemy."

I wait as the two sit back down and confer in Italian. I can understand every word, but I simply sit there pretending to be oblivious.

"Look, the incoming account numbers match, the amounts match, and the transaction times match, too. I know this Steele guy's supposed to have serious balls, but he wouldn't just show us stuff that sensitive when it could fuck him later, unless he really did believe it would get us off his neck." Scarface rubs his face, loosening his collar. His cheeks are pink. The Scotch is doing its work.

The behemoth nods slowly. *"Look, cousin, we don't get paid to bring trouble to the wrong door. But you know that if we don't find the Boss a scapegoat soon, he's probably gonna take this out on us."*

"He's not gonna do that, Joey, we're made men. He'll give us time to find the right guy." But Scarface has his doubts. I can see it in his eyes.

"But what happens if we can't find the right guy?"

Scarface cuts his eyes over to me as I smile blandly. *"Then we give him the convenient guy."*

Once they are gone, I pour the two fingers of Glenmorangie left in the bottle into my own glass and savor it, breathing deep as I find my center again. I call the desk to have them stand down the alert, and then call John.

"There's a good chance that Marcone will be sending a cleaning crew after my hand within the next week." My voice is low and hard, and I hear him suck air.

"I half expected it tonight when you brought us up to a Code Six. The helicopter's fueled and prepped on the rooftop, lethal rounds were distributed, and we have reinforcements and medical personnel on standby."

"All right. Drop it down to a Code Four for now. Keep the damn helicopter ready unless wind speeds endanger her. I'll fly her out of here myself if it comes down to it. I want reinforcements kept on-call, but let them go home and get some sleep." I take another sip of Scotch.

"I want supervisors only to keep their lethals and check the others in the exterior duty lockers. I don't want any nervous rookies getting trigger-happy." I rub my chin. "I'm going to be keeping my panic button handy just in case."

Some men have panic rooms. I have a panic penthouse. The outer doors bolt like a bank vault when it goes on lock-down, the armored window glass polarizes to prevent snipers from attempting a lock on my location, and I have an escape tunnel that leads to the helipad above us.

I have food stores and essentials for six months, including luxuries—from toiletries to massage oil to my wine cellar. I have solar- and wind-charged house batteries backing up my power, a satellite uplink to ensure connectivity, and an emergency water tank that could last up to a month for five people. If Marcone's goons think I'm a convenient target, they'll soon realize how wrong they are.

"So, while we're preparing, what are you going to do?" John is typing away at something while we talk. I assume he's e-mailing his four assistants.

"I'm going to enlist the hacker who started this mess to throw Marcone off the scent. She led him to my door," I say firmly, trying to ignore how the prospect of bringing Robin here, alone—*tonight*—excites me. "She can damn well lead him away again."

CHAPTER 9

Robin

I try not to stare as I walk into Drake's museum of a penthouse, but it's tough. I've never seen anything like this place. The ceiling soars up twenty feet to a series of domes set with mirrored mosaics and inset lights; each dome is supported by towering pillars of polished wood. The floor is an acre of elaborately inlaid wood, with scattered islands of furniture and thick Persian rugs.

Aside from the bathroom, his whole life is on display—the breakfast alcove beside the stainless steel and copper kitchen, the indoor jacuzzi, the sprawling black-sheeted bed. Out front, greeting everyone coming in the main door, is his enormous steel and wood battleship of a desk, which he's standing beside as I walk in.

"Thank you for coming so quickly," he says tiredly, and I feel a stab of guilt that pulls me out of my reverie. "You said you were willing to do what it took to get Marcone off my back, and it seems we're short on time."

"I will," I walk over slowly, rubbing the corners of my eyes. He's already briefed me on his encounter with Marcone's goons. "I wouldn't have risked coming here if I wasn't committed."

"Good to know. Though for the record, this place is set up to withstand a siege from a small army." He sounds proud, and I look back at the huge doors I just walked through.

"I can believe it." I look around again. "What's your escape route?"

"Hidden passage to the rooftop where there's a helipad. I fly out." He seems to want to reassure me that I am safe here. That I can safely *stay* here, even if Marcone's men end up on the hunt for both of us.

Maybe he wants me to stay. At least for a while.

I glance over at the enormous bed with its carved wood frame and towering posts. "You...don't seem entirely set up for guests here," I murmur.

"I've only ever had lovers here overnight," he admits, his dark lashes shading his eyes briefly. "But...if things don't turn in that direction, I do have a comfortable couch."

"I've slept on a lot worse," I say gamely, and he chuckles and shakes his head.

"If this hacking job I need you to do on Marcone goes long enough that we need rest, you're taking my bed." His smile broadens, going just a touch sly. "Whether I'm in it as well or not, I'll leave up to you."

Both his gallantry and his bald flirtation startle me into silence. My cheeks start prickling again. *Damn it.*

"I'm surprised you're not angry at me," I admit cautiously. I'm still waiting for the hook in all the bait he's waving—the trap behind these strange, perilously distracting good feelings.

"If you had not come right over to fix this as you promised, then I'd be angry at you. But you did, and here you are. And besides, even if I was angry at you, I know you would do the right thing eventually."

He's staring into my eyes. My mouth is so dry. I suddenly realize that I never did take a seat across the desk, and instead I'm simply standing there with him, closer than I realized.

It suddenly feels like unseen arcs of warm electricity are running back and forth between us, drawing me toward him. He moves a touch closer, bending down over me just slightly. "I haven't misread you, have I?" he asks almost tenderly, and my heart suddenly aches.

"N—no." I suck in a deep breath, feeling exhilarated and scared at the same time. I want him to be close to me, but I'm not used to being touched anymore. Physical contact still feels hazardous after so many years alone.

I fight to stay cool and just let this...happen. But then a few seconds later, I start to feel overwhelmed. The fear starts to win.

He sees it and moves back slightly. I look shyly over at his computer setup. "We should...get to work," I say softly.

He nods, smiling, and gestures to his chair.

I feel like a kid in his enormous brown leather executive's chair. I sink into its deep cushions, its softness easing the aches in my back that I had simply gotten used to having there.

So much luxury. It's the one thing I don't like about Drake so far. He loves the finer things so much.

I don't know whether he grew up in a family like mine where a certain amount of opulence was expected. Or maybe he had nothing and always wanted a luxurious, secure home. But I can't help but look around and think about how that Calder mobile would fund a shelter for ten years. That Picasso—twenty.

Still, I'm the idiot who rides a cheap desk chair all day and has a backache because I didn't get the best, so maybe I'm too austere for my own good.

"So, what's the plan?" He looms behind me, one hand spread on his desktop near where I'm using the mouse. I can feel the warmth from his hand on the side of mine. I breathe slowly and lightly, doing my best to hide just how much I like it.

Focus. "They want a convenient target. What about Yoshida? He's likely to come looking for Marcone anyway." I am cracking my way into Marcone's private accounts again. Not just banks and Bitcoin repositories, but everything.

"I don't know. I have reservations against supporting any effort against Yoshida that he might trace back to me. Right now, it looks like he robbed me, and I'm not complaining to him."

I bite down lightly on my lip with a mix of frustration and worry. "Well, who else can we shift the blame to?"

"What about just spoofing the account?" He's moved even closer. If I wasn't interested—if he hadn't clearly figured out that I'm interested—it would feel creepy as hell to have him this close. "Convince him that the money is still there, and that its missing status was just a temporary glitch?"

I lick my lips, flustered and now even more frustrated. "I'm sorry but you're not getting it. It's almost impossible to clone Bitcoin in the way you're asking unless it's as a temporary measure."

I'm not used to working under observation. Between his raw masculine presence and the way he's hovering, it's distracting as hell. "If we don't find a fall guy, we need to make them think the authorities are messing with them."

"I don't want to drag anyone else into this," he insists. "I thought you were talented. But you're telling me now that you can't find a way to peacefully resolve this by adjusting numbers in Marcone's accounts?"

I get up, furious, and turn and step close to confront him. "What I'm telling you is that it can't be done on a short timetable! Riding my ass isn't going to change that. I thought you knew this business."

I remember that getting so close is a mistake, but for a moment I'm so pissed I don't fully remember why. Not until my breasts brush against his chest, and I feel his warm breath on my face.

I take a huge breath of my own. "If not Yoshida, and if not some other deserving scumbag, then who do we get Marcone to blame for this? Even if I clone those same Bitcoin back into his account and his people write it off as a mistake for a while, eventually those fakes will vanish as soon as the blockchain is updated."

"So, you *can* trick him?"

I put my hands on my hips. "I can do it, and it will buy us time, but that's it!"

"Then do it," he growls, voice husky as his hands brush against the backs of mine. "We need to buy time, or we'll never be able to sort this out."

"F—fine," I manage, my heart banging away in my ears again. I settle back down into the seat, my whole body thrumming from the brief contact. My mind is so hazy that I have to catch my breath before I can get back to work.

Is he seducing me? I shiver. *I'm so scared of being hurt.*

But would it hurt more than it does now? Could anything be worse than my days alone and my empty nights? Maybe he can make that emptiness go away for a while, instead of hurting me.

I set my jaw and force myself to focus. *You're not his type. He's a rich man who lives in a palace on top of a skyscraper. You're a green-haired cyberpunk who used to live in a box.*

It doesn't take too long before I have all of Don Marcone's online life spread out before us. "This is it," I say quietly. "Every bit of dirty laundry—his medical records, all his accounts. From here, I can do a lot. It's your call."

He is behind me now, one hand on my shoulder as we look over what I've found. I struggle to stay professional but wish his hand would wander further. The tap of the rain against the window reminds me of the many icy nights I spent alone, and I want to feel the heat from his hand all through me, to drive those cold memories away.

You have a job to do, I remind myself, and keep typing.

"All right. The police won't move fast enough for my tastes, but if you leak to them where to find some of this information, our friend Rocco will end up even busier."

I start sending e-mails to the police's anonymous tip account with as much information on Marcone as I can grab. Transfers to his offshore accounts, incriminating e-mails...and from his hard drive, some nude images of suspiciously young girls. "What about leaking some information to Yoshida as well?"

"Hmm. Yoshida will be coming after him no matter what we do. He believes that the Don stole from him. Yoshida is more likely to be an immediate problem for Marcone than the police, but if he traces any of this back to us...that's *two* enemies I don't need."

I look up at him, getting annoyed again. "He won't. He'll trace it where I want, just like Marcone did."

"I would believe that...except that you're not uncatchable." His tone almost sounds apologetic, but it still stings. "I already proved that, remember?"

Another surge of anger rushes through me, and I shoot a glare his way. "I reached out to you, remember?"

"And by the time you did, I already knew your name, your history, and had a good idea of what you looked like." Now he just sounds condescending—and worse, he's right, which just pisses me off more.

His other hand settles on my shoulder. "Marcone is an idiot.

He is easily led. But like me, Dr. Yoshida is not an idiot. I cannot afford to underestimate him."

That electric energy flows from his hands into me, making me shiver with primal need even as what he's saying pisses me off. I keep typing, finishing spoofing the Don's accounts and "refilling" them with phantom money.

Finally, I sit back. Done. Right now, the police are getting the Don's dirty laundry, the Don's account is being padded with phantom money, and my crawlers are looking for even more dirt on him. That knowledge helps me calm down enough to deal with Drake.

I get up, turning to challenge him again, but I'm calmer this time. More aware of his effect on me. "No, he's not an idiot. But an anonymous e-mail with the list I just found two minutes ago will help make sure the Don's too busy running from Yoshida to worry about us."

His eyes narrow slightly as he stands his ground. "What have you got?"

"It looks suspiciously like a list of local mob safe houses. If this gets to Yoshida, that big scumbag Marcone won't have anywhere to hide." I'm proud to have found it on such short notice.

But even though he's towering over me, eyelids at half-mast and a little shake sounding in the bottom of his breath, even though I can feel the heat of his body through our clothes because we're standing so close, he looks neither distracted nor impressed.

If anything, he looks skeptical. "I'll think about it."

"That's it?" Now I'm really getting annoyed. "You'll think about it."

"Yes." He looks down firmly into my eyes, that faint smile teasing his lips again. "You have set the delays in place as I requested. I won't move hastily on a permanent solution—that is what caused this problem in the first place."

It's true—and again, it stings more for being true. I glare up at him, my mouth working.

His expression softens as he catches the look in my eyes. "I'm not saying these things to humiliate you, Robin. I'm just saying... we can't be hasty."

"I just want this guy gone," I mumble, looking down. "I want to make sure he doesn't hurt you because of what I did, damn it. You think I like the idea that Marcone might send more goons before we can even try to convince him to look elsewhere?"

"If he does, he does. This place is protected. And I'm going to do everything I can to make sure," he tucks some of my stray hairs behind my ear as he leans over me intimately, "that even if he comes here with a fucking tank, the two of us will be safe from him."

I'm trembling. I should pull away. I hold still.

"Why are you doing this?" I gasp, finally managing to move back from him a little.

He blinks at me a few times before leaning on his desk. "You've never had someone flirt with you? Not catcalling, not anything creepy, but just flirt with you?"

I stare at him, at a loss, and finally mutter, "I don't interact with people much anymore. But...no. On the streets, lone girls avoid men. And after that, I was...busy."

It sounds like a cop-out, but I don't want to go into detail—that painful mix of loneliness and fear that battles inside of me whenever I think of men and sex.

I can't remember being flirted with by anyone who wasn't either kidding or trying to exploit me. Spider and most of his boys were gay. Nobody who approached me while I was homeless had good intentions. And men on the internet seem to enjoy being as disgusting as possible.

The incentive to make a connection has never been there for me. The incentive to stay cautiously alone always has been.

But when *he* stands near me—when he touches me—I want him to do it more. It scares me. Can I trust myself? This feeling? Him? Is it safe?

I suddenly find myself silently blinking back tears.

"Hey," he says, worry crossing his face as he straightens again and moves toward me, gently raising a hand. His voice is soft. "I didn't mean to make you cry."

I sniffle and hold up my hands, mortified. "Look, I...you're attractive, and if you're really the kind of guy you seem to be now that I'm getting to know you, I could learn to trust you. But I'm just not there yet."

My voice cracks. I look away, totally humiliated. Staring out at the city, I mutter almost angrily. "Guys like you don't understand what it's like to go through what I have. You live in a palace. You fly a helicopter. You spend the kind of money I took from you on a weekend shopping spree."

"Guys like me?" He scoffs and drags over a chair to sit down beside me as I settle back into his desk chair. "You have no idea what I'm like, except for what I have let you see."

"And yet you expect me to trust you," I retort.

He sits back...and then smiles wryly. "You know what? You're right. Ask me whatever you want to know."

I relax, starting to feel a little intrigued myself. "Fine. Uh..."

I open my mouth to ask him who he used to launder money for, when suddenly an alarm shrills somewhere deep in the building. Drake's phone rings at the same time.

He stiffens, a hard, wary gleam coming into his eyes as he pulls out his phone. "Hold that thought."

CHAPTER 10

Drake

I'm finally getting somewhere with both the Marcone problem and Robin's trust issues when all hell breaks loose. "What is it?" I snap as I answer my phone.

I already know. Just not the specifics.

"Drake, they busted through the bollards and armored glass with a tractor trailer. They're inside." I hear John shouting over the shrilling alarm. "Twelve men that we know of!"

Fuck. "Marcone's men?"

"Safe bet, though they're in ski masks. Your orders?"

In the back of my head I start swearing in Russian and making plans. Nasty plans. "Condition Omega. Scatter into three-man teams, pick them off using guerrilla tactics, track them constantly on the security cameras to stay agile. Do not get close to them. I can't afford to have anyone taken hostage.

"Do not make a stand at the penthouse. If they get up this far, lock them in, put the elevator out of service and call the police to pick them up. Let my panic doors do their job. If they somehow find a way through, the helicopter is prepped."

My voice has gone cold, and I hear the faintest return of my accent. It happens when I'm under enough stress, and right now I want to kick ass and don't have a deserving target nearby. "I want updates every minute. Text if you can't talk." I hang up.

"Oh God." Robin is shivering next to me, her lovely face showing the terror of a trapped animal.

One glance at the haunted, familiar look of despair in her eyes, and my rage gets shoved aside by something far more urgent. I can't stand seeing it. It stuns me that she's gotten under my skin this much already, but I go with it.

I turn to her and hug her gently, cradling her head in my palm as I draw her against my chest. "It's okay. Stay calm. I've prepared for this."

She stiffens in my grip. Then a long shudder goes through her as she digs her fingers into my shirtfront and buries her face in my chest. "What do we do?"

I pet her hair gently until she calms down enough to look up at me. "Building's going on lock-down, and I'm armed. Do you know how to use a pistol?"

She shakes her head, looking embarrassed.

"All right then, here's the deal. They are not breaking in here. The only way that we can possibly come in contact with them is if they intercept us on the way out." I want to hold her again, comfort her more, but she's nodding, snapping out of it already —and there's no time.

"Should we just fly out and leave them trying to get into an empty penthouse?" she asks, and I stop to consider. She isn't handling the prospect of waiting out a siege well. If I give a damn, I shouldn't ask her to stay, even if I'm fine with it.

"Get your coat on. The temperature's dropping pretty fast." Past the polarized windows, I can see the rain turning into thin swirls of snow. "I've got a safe house in the Hamptons. I'll fly us over there and let the police and security mop up here."

She nods and goes to take her coat out of the closet by the entry door, moving shakily. I already miss her warm, slight body against me. But once we're in the Hamptons...perhaps she'll want to celebrate our escape.

John buzzes me again. "We've disabled two and trapped two more in sealed rooms. The police are en route. I've directed their 'copter to the far side of our helipad. Ten minutes."

"Good. Keep at it." I look up to see Robin wrapping herself in that camel-colored coat. "Okay," I call over to her. "Pack up the computers while I get my gun. We're out of here."

She smiles and nods, hurrying back to the desk. "Thank you." The relief on her face does me a world of good.

Apparently, my heart doesn't care if her hair's green either.

I turn to my gun safe and pull out my shoulder holster and Berettas, strapping them on. "I have been in too many dangerous situations," I explain. "I forget that what I see as a fortress may feel like a trap to someone else."

The phone rings. John again. "Update?" I ask—just as I hear the heavy thrum of a helicopter approaching.

"We've got a helicopter coming in to land from the northeast. Can't get a clear look at it in all this snow, but the police gave me a pretty fast ETA."

I frown. Something about this seems off. But if the police have shown up early and want to trap Marcone's men between two teams, it's not a bad plan. "Try and raise that chopper to give them landing clearance; we'll hole up until they've set down."

I hang up and see Robin has packed the two laptop bags and is hugging mine to her chest like a shield. "Okay, the cops are landing on the roof. I want you to follow me, but not too closely. They might ask us to shelter in place until they're done with their roundup."

She nods and follows me as I go over to the mirrored wall beside my home gym. I press a hidden panel and a section of mirror slides back and aside with a click. Beyond, a tight spiral staircase ascends into the dark.

I check with John. "Are they ready for us?"

"They've touched down," comes the reply. "Rotors are powering off."

"On our way then. I'll call you back when we're clear of the building." I hang up. I'm aware of my pistols as I come up the stairs with Robin behind me, but I don't draw them. If the cops see me with a firearm in hand, they may shoot first.

"Hang back a bit," I murmur to her as I reach the top and unlatch the heavy steel door.

I don't know what makes me feel so cautious as I duck my head around the low, curved door frame. Maybe it's that, aside from Robin's presence, the night's been a total shit-show. Maybe it's because Robin is close behind me, and I'm still thinking of her safety.

And I've never trusted cops much either. Cops can be biased. They can drop a tank on one man and slap the other on the back of the hand for the same crime. They can also be bribed.

I see four figures moving toward me from the dark hulk of the second helicopter, and for a moment, I start to lift a hand in greeting. But then I see the gleam of weapons in their hands as they raise them.

And apparently police helicopters can be stolen!

"Fuck!" I duck back inside, clawing my pistol from its holster. "Get back—it's not the cops!"

Robin lets out a cry of dismay, and I hear her bolt back down the stairs. *Good girl.*

Now to deal with my unwanted guests.

I hear running feet coming toward us, and I fire blind around the corner—hearing grunts and yelling. I empty my other Beretta the same way, hearing a sharp cry and a few curses. Then I hear those booted feet scramble for cover.

It's a relief, but there's something I didn't want Robin to realize. We're actually in some trouble.

If I lock us in, they'll take off again and fire on the windows. If I let them in, they'll have a chance to hurt Robin, and that can't happen. I weigh my options as I reload, unimpressed by all of them.

Unless...

The shooting has stopped. I duck my head around to check my bearings—and nearly get pegged between the eyes. *Ugh, sneaky bastards!*

But the risk I took does the job; I know what to do now. I fire blind again—but angle my shots carefully, hearing them bite into the side of the helicopter.

A heavy patter and glug of liquid, and a whole lot of cursing in Italian, tell me that I've hit the bullseye. No way to take off with a hole in the fuel tank and my helicopter is impossible to hot-wire—though I'm guessing they're about to waste a lot of time trying it while their butts freeze off.

I GRAB the door and slam it shut, leaving the cursing mobsters on the other side. The stink of cordite fills the stairway. I hold my breath and holster my guns.

I come back down laughing. "They're locked on the roof with no way down until the police get to them," I say as I step out of the secret door and close it behind me. My ears still echo with gunfire; I feel a little giddy.

Robin is staring at me. She's set the computer bags down on the desk and walks over to me slowly, worry breaking over her face.

I hesitate. "What is it?"

"You're bleeding,"

I look down at myself—and see that there's a hole under the arm of my suit jacket, and finally feel that something underneath stings. Blood is seeping slowly through the fabric. "Oh."

Damn.

CHAPTER 11

Robin

The suddenly intensifying snowstorm is delaying the police. There are mobsters trapped on the roof, and more mobsters are trapped in the building. We have no way out...but we can outlast them.

I keep telling myself all of this as I sit Drake down on the edge of his huge bathtub and gingerly peel off his suit coat, shirt, and undershirt. Every layer has tears in it where the bullet passed through. I try not to stare at his massively muscled, tattooed torso as I toss the cloth in the sink and peer closely at the wound.

"How bad is it?" he grunts as he lifts his arm.

I examine it a moment and then lean back, surprised and a bit more hopeful. He didn't exactly dodge the bullet, but...close enough.

"Not bad at all. It's long and shallow and already clotting. But it has to be disinfected, and it will probably have a bruise around it." I'm trying to be brave. Blood really isn't something I'm used to dealing with. But I really want to help. "How are your ribs?"

He takes an experimentally deep breath. "Little sore. Might have cracked one, but I've got no sharp pains, and no trouble breathing. An inch to the left though, and the bullet would have taken a chunk out of me."

"I'm just glad you were lucky." I take off my coat and boots, knowing we won't be going anywhere, and toss them aside before crouching in front of him to examine the wound more closely. Then I reach into the first aid kit I retrieved from the closet and take out some alcohol swabs.

He sits quietly while I tend to him, not wincing or flinching once.

"So, you're Russian," I comment as I gently clean the wound.

"Yes, I was born in Moscow. And before you ask, I'm not part of any *bratva* anymore." His Russian is so perfect that it turns even that one word into music. "But I needed their protection as a teenager in prison, and it took me many years to buy my way out."

My heart sinks with unexpected sympathy. *He had no choice?* That certainly seems to fit with what I have seen of his character, more than the idea that he's a particularly fluent liar. But then again…I'm biased.

"I see. There are still rumors around that you're an active member of…something." The wound bleeds a little bit as I clean it, but it's more a long, ugly scrape than anything serious. "Don't think I can judge you for making a deal, especially if you were a kid when you went inside. Russian prisons are infamous."

"They are indeed," he rumbles in a low, tired voice. But I can see relief on his face. Was he that worried that I would judge him? *Happy to disappoint.*

I've learned my lesson about jumping to negative conclusions about Drake Steele.

I wash the blood off of him gently, fascinated by the smooth ripple of muscle up his side. "How does that feel?" I murmur distractedly.

"Your nursing skills are top-notch," he purrs in response, and I reluctantly straighten. "This history of mine...it doesn't bother you?"

I have to think about it before answering him, so maybe it does a little. In the end, though, I admit the truth. "I always knew you had a past. I just didn't know what it was." My tone is more tender than I want it to be, but less tender than I feel. "I guess we both have histories we're trying to get away from."

He stares at me intensely for a few moments and then stands, towering half-naked over me. I straighten, looking up at him—and he takes me in his arms. "I'm glad you understand."

Oh my God, he's half-naked. I freeze and look up at him—and feel his heart beating fast against my breasts. "I'm surprised," I mumble, my fingertips trailing shyly up his chest. "I...I got you shot."

"No, I got me shot. I should have waited until we confirmed their damn identities before opening the roof access." His huge hand strokes back through my hair, and I feel the muscles in my neck loosen at the caress.

I want to melt into his arms all of a sudden. We're trapped in here, and it might be hours before we can leave. It scares me—stifles me. Waiting for a police rescue almost feels like a joke... but I'm inside a fortress right now. Safe. With him.

I want him to drown out this caged feeling that I just can't get rid of. I throw my arms around his neck and lean against him—and his mouth comes down on mine and steals my breath.

His lips and tongue work against mine insistently, teasing out my response until I'm kissing him back just as fiercely. I'm clumsy, nervous; I've got no clue what I'm doing. My legs wobble, and he scoops me up against him. I cling to him like a rock in a storm.

His mouth tastes like a mix of coffee, brandy, and mint, and he holds me in a grip that's too firm to break, but doesn't hurt at all. I feel the play of his lips against mine all the way down to my thighs, and suddenly I can't catch my breath.

Oh my God, I never imagined... It's like someone shot me full of a drug I've never heard of, waking up every inch of my skin, leaving me filled with pleasure and thirsty for more. I whimper against his lips, my heartbeat in my ears, my back arching to press more of myself against him.

When the kiss breaks, he backs off just a little and looks down at me, breathing heavily. One hand cups my jaw. "You all right?" he asks me, very gently checking in.

It's his tenderness that reassures me more than anything, despite the scary newness of it all. If he was faking...why bother? Why not just push me into it?

I smile at him shyly and nod, and he kisses me again even more fiercely.

Then his damned phone goes off again.

"Shit. John. It slipped my mind for a moment." He smiles at me, winks, and pulls out his phone. "Hi. I'm alive. Those weren't the police, though."

I can hear a man's voice faintly through the speaker. "Yeah, I have them on the line asking for clearance. Looks like Marcone's boys used their own 'copter. They slapped on some dummy decals, and we couldn't see them clearly in the storm. Are you all right?"

"I got hit, but it was just a graze. Probably won't need stitches even, but I should have the ribs X-rayed later. I do have to tend to this, though..." He looks me over with heat in his eyes, and his grip around my waist tightened slightly. "As well as some related unfinished business. Any problems downstairs?"

"One of the men got hit in the vest. He's bruised and lost his supper, but he's conscious. Every other casualty is on their side, and they're trapped now."

Drake smiles. "Good. Keep up the good work. From now on, contact me only if there's an emergency, or when the police actually arrive."

"That could be a while. The 'copters just got grounded by snow, and the streets may be impassable soon." I hear the man chuckle. "We've turned off heating in the section the goons are trapped in. That should soften them up just like the boys on the roof."

"Sounds like they're in for a long, cold wait!" He laughs as he hangs up. I can't help but smile as well.

Tucking his phone back into his pocket, he looks down at me, and his smile goes lopsided. "How about we make our own wait a lot hotter?"

I've never done this. I have to push my self-consciousness down...but I want this so damned bad. And the fact that he wants it as well makes me braver. "If...they really can't get in..."

He smooths my hair back. "They really can't get in."

I smile softly. "Okay." *Then drown out the world for me.*

This time his kiss is softer, lingering, teasing at my lips, making me chase his. His playfulness eases my nerves. I giggle —and then he silences me with his mouth.

My hands start exploring his back, learning the way it tenses and flexes under my fingertips, the smooth skin, the slick patches of scars. I wonder how many fights he's survived if he's treating being grazed by a bullet so casually. It feels like a lot.

His fingers are busy unbuttoning my blouse while his mouth ravages mine. I want this. I want his big, rough hands sliding over my skin—and when I slip out of the blouse and feel just that, I moan with delight.

His hands slide up and down my back, over my sides, my arms, my belly...and then up to cup my breasts. He kneads them softly through the fabric of my bra as I relax against him, then he tugs the cups upward a little and slides his hands inside.

The feel of his fingertips brushing against my nipple almost hurts; a rush of sensation overloads my nerves, and I whimper and bite my lip hard. He nuzzles my cheek, and then nibbles his way back along my jawline and up my chin before teasing me into another kiss.

Every stroke of his fingers over that sensitive skin makes my muscles tighten. I shake, knees clenched together, my cunt starting to ache. Then his hands slide back behind me to unfasten my bra, and he tugs it off my shoulders as I squirm to help get it off. I have to fight off the shy urge to hold the cloth over my breasts, but I'm determined now. I want more.

His eyes light up fiercely as the cool air hits my breasts, and my nipples tighten almost painfully under his gaze. I've always been self-conscious about my body, but the hungry way he's staring at me helps...a lot. But I'm not quite ready for what happens next.

He scoops me up, arms around my waist, and starts covering my chest with kisses—between and under my breasts, then all over them. He grunts a little as my thigh hits his wound, but a shift of position fixes his discomfort, and he goes right back to what he was doing.

I dig my nails into his shoulders and cry out sharply as I feel his tongue play over my nipple. Then his mouth closes over it, and a long, warm, rough pull makes my voice rise to a scream.

I squirm, not sure whether to pull away or push closer, my nerves overloaded. He pushes me back against the wall, pins me there, my breasts pillowed against his face as he sucks and licks and nibbles greedily. My voice is out of control; I can hear it echoing off the walls, my cries growing more desperate over time.

Don't stop...

He groans against my breast, his fingers digging into my ass cheeks as he holds me up. My skirt has rucked up past my hips, leaving only my wool tights between my flesh and his hands. He starts to knead my ass as he pins me against the wall, his thighs and shoulders taking my weight as if it's nothing.

I cling to him, crooning, and then my voice rises sharply again as he starts suckling my other breast. His hands knead me firmly; the ache inside me is gathering into a knot deep inside my cunt. The sensation leaves me dizzy and drunk—I need more sensation, but what I'm experiencing already is driving me wild.

He shifts his grip on me, and then starts carrying me toward that massive bed, moving easily. My head is swimming, the brief reprieve relieving me and disappointing me at the same time. My breath comes in little whimpering sips, and as he settles me down on the broad mattress, I squirm against its velvet coverlet and reach for him pleadingly.

He stands back, out of reach, and slowly removes his clothes. His actions are almost meditative, except for the burning heat in his eyes—and the enormous bulge in his crotch that I can't easily look away from.

His legs are as powerfully muscled as the rest of him, crossed here and there with more faint scars. When he unzips and slides out of trousers and boxers at the same time and steps forward, his sleek, uncut length bounces free of his fly, and I reach out for it greedily.

The skin is silky, and I run my fingers over it. He stiffens and sucks air. I start to stroke him, intrigued at how even a gentle touch can make him shake. He lets out a soft grunt and gently pushes my hands away.

"You first," he rasps huskily, moving forward to pull off my skirt.

He's almost dainty in the way he rolls my tights down and lays aside my skirt. His warm hands slide over the bare skin of my legs as he frees them from the tights…and then he parts my thighs and moves up in between them, running his mouth up the inside of one in a way that makes my toes curl.

His breath is warm as it blows over my mound, and then his long fingers are sliding in between my lips, slowly starting to explore. I let out a low sob, lifting my hips—and he stuns me completely when he lowers his head and kisses my cunt tenderly.

His tongue darts between my lips and starts to meander up and down, exploring every fold of me…and then works its way upward, bit by tantalizing bit. My eyes fly open as I feel him kiss nearer and nearer to my aching, neglected clit—and then he pounces, and starts lashing his tongue over and around it firmly.

My head snaps back and I wail, grabbing handfuls of the covers, pushing up on my heels as I roll my hips against his face. He feasts on me, the long, swirling strokes of his tongue growing firmer and faster as time goes on, until I feel the muscles of my cunt tighten.

Everything catches fire—ecstasy rockets through me, exploding outward in waves through my body while I scream and thrash as he holds me down. It's so good that I almost blackout for a moment, washed away on a tide of pleasure. And still he keeps tonguing me mercilessly, up until the point where I collapse and feel him climbing onto the mattress over me.

He seizes my hips, pushes my knees up and apart, and settles over me. His powerful weight makes the springs creak. I feel the push of his cock against me—and then he's sliding into my slick, tingling wetness. Being filled sets off aftershocks in my body, which only intensify as he groans and starts to thrust.

I sob, clinging to him, overwhelmed in the best way possible, as he drives against me hard enough to push me deep into the mattress. He shouts with pleasure every time he sinks into me, his voice deep and hoarse. I croon and clutch at him, feeling my body tingle with pleasure at each fresh jolt.

He's tireless, feral, his voice hoarse in my ear as he moves against me endlessly. I'm going to explode again.

I start to squirm under him, rolling my hips up to meet his. He gasps through his teeth and starts pounding harder. I look up and see his back arched, head thrown back, his every muscle taut. Then his cock jolts inside me—and the sudden movement sets me off.

I thrash mutely this time, my muscles clenching around his shaft—which jumps and shudders inside me as he pants and shouts with bliss. We pull each other so close it's like we're trying to become one...and then relax, gasping softly for air.

He collapses over me, completely spent. Low groans escape him with every breath, and he shivers when I stroke my hands up and down his back. Inside of me, his cock is dwindling, and as we both catch our breath, I have to smile at myself.

That was definitely worth taking the risk, I think, and stroke his hair as he dozes, enjoying his warm weight pushing me into the mattress.

We drowse together for a while before I wake to find him bundling us in under the covers. He yawns in my ear as he curls up behind me and wraps an arm over me. "Get some rest," he purrs in my ear. "I'm definitely not done with you yet."

I smile, and murmur sleepily, "That's the best news I've heard all night."

CHAPTER 12

Drake

As it turned out, it took six hours for the storm let up and the streets to clear enough for the police to come collect all our half-frozen mobsters. Marcone himself went missing—word on the street says that Yoshida is after him along with the police.

Which is why my dear little Robin and I leaked the list of safe house addresses to the both of them.

Two weeks later, and he's still hiding. We've got a bet running on who will find him first. I say the police; she says Yoshida. We'll see who wins—the loser gets blindfolded and tied to a bed. Which is another way of winning, but we both like leaving it to chance.

Not so the fate of her twenty thousand or the displaced tenants who were once her neighbors. I've been helping Robin with that, as has my team. The more that we get done, the more free time she has—for me.

It's around midnight, and we're in bed again after a long day of saving lives with my money. The marks from her nails still sting my back, and she's a warm, soft, sleepy ball curled against my chest. My nose is buried in her hair as I listen to her soft breathing.

I've never been more content in my life.

I haven't had any nightmares since before our first night together. The kid in that prison yard is done growing up, and something in my head has finally sorted out that I'm free of that place for good. Now maybe my heart can move on, just as the rest of my life has.

Now and again, though, Robin still has nightmares of her own, and cries softly in her sleep. She's told me about the box that served as her shelter, and the men in the alley, and how alone she felt then. I've decided to make sure that she never feels that way again.

It's so strange that we switched places in our lives: the heiress turned thief, and the thief turned wealthy man. Yet somehow, we work together.

We have a lot to do. There are people to save—and people to get revenge on. I'm already planning to cause some trouble for her uncle, who has been sending her several nervous, unanswered messages since the first paparazzi photos of the pair of us together started making the rounds.

He must recognize me. And he must know that in me, Robin has an ally far more powerful than her uncle ever dreamed. That's big trouble for him.

I wonder how he's sleeping. Probably not well.

I'm settling back in and closing my eyes when my phone buzzes on the shelf beside my bed. I reach for it as Robin stirs.

It's a message from John. As she uncurls and rolls toward me, stretching against my body, I read the text, and smirk.

Marcone gave himself up to police after receiving a...

request...from Yoshida regarding the return of his missing Bitcoin. It was apparently delivered to one of his safe houses by courier. He's asking for protection.

I start laughing, and Robin yawns and stretches against me, blinking up at me curiously. "What is it?"

"You're not going to believe this, but..." I show her. "Looks like our little bet ends in a tie!"

She scratches behind her ear, her emerald hair mussed with sleep. It's growing on me, though I don't think I'll be sporting the merman look myself anytime soon.

She starts snickering as she reads the text. "If it's a tie, though, who gets tied?"

I rumble contentedly and nuzzle her cheek, then lie back and draw her slight form over me. "We'll have to take turns."

It's a cold world out there; we're both intimately familiar with that. But we're making our own warmth together. I still hate being stolen from—but if I get Robin in return, she can take as much from me as she wants.

The End.

©Copyright 2020 by Michelle Love - All rights Reserved
In no way is it legal to reproduce, duplicate, or transmit any part of this document in either electronic means or in printed format. Recording of this publication is strictly prohibited and any storage of this document is not allowed unless with written permission from the publisher. All rights are reserved.
Respective authors own all copyrights not held by the publisher.

 Created with Vellum

www.ingramcontent.com/pod-product-compliance
Lightning Source LLC
LaVergne TN
LVHW021943060526
838200LV00042B/1913